Friendship or Foul Play
Taylor Takes Her Shot
Step-by-Step series

Paul Breau

Cover illustrated by
Rose Gulhan

l

Published by TKI Productions, Inc.

Friendship or Foul Play is a work of fiction. Names, characters, businesses, places, events, locales, and incidents are either the products of the author's imagination or used in a fictitious manner. Any resemblance to actual persons, living or dead, or actual events is purely coincidental.

Text copyright © 2022 by Paul Breau

First paperback edition in this format 2022
Book art design by Rose Gulhan

ISBN 978-1-7779766-0-6 (paperback)
ISBN 978-1-7779766-1-3 (electronic book)
ISBN 978-1-7779766-2-0 (audio)

www.PaulBreau.com

CONTENTS

DEDICATION

For Sienna and Jenn
Thank you for being the best part of my story.

Extra Special Thanks
Ryan Murphy
Chelsey B
Kristen Chavez

NO SUCH THING AS FRIENDLY

There was no such thing as a friendly basketball game in my world. You played hard, and you played to win. Even if that meant stealing the basketball from your best friend.

In my case, that would be Melina. We'd been best friends for years. She was a good basketball player, but she telegraphed all her moves. It was her biggest weakness. If you paid attention, which I always did, you could tell exactly what she was going to do next.

Sure enough, Melina shifted her weight to the right. Her plan was to throw the ball between my legs, catch it on the other side, and make a run for the basket. Or at least try.

Unfortunately, there was a huge problem with her plan. Me.

It was my signature move, and it definitely wasn't going to work against me. Not now. Not ever. I was taller and faster than Melina and my arms were longer. And I was patient.

Her eyes glanced left and then down at my feet. I waited until the last possible second to move, but as soon as she thrust the ball, I dropped low and blocked it with my arm.

Grabbing the ball, I dashed toward the hoop. One, two, three strides, and I went up for the easy layup.

At least, I thought it was going to be easy.

As I flew through the air, a chill ran down my spine and the hairs on my arms and the back of my neck stood up.

The strange sensation threw me completely off my game. I lost control of the ball, and it spun awkwardly out my hand and clanged hard against the rim of the basket.

I landed ready for the rebound, but the ball took a bad bounce off a rough patch of pavement.

As I watched it roll away, I couldn't shake the odd feeling. Basketball was usually the one thing in my life I had control over. Sure, I'd missed plenty of shots before, but this was different. Something felt off.

I shook my head and walked over to the stray ball.

"Taylor!" Melina called. "How do you always know what I'm going to do?"

"You've got a tell."

"What's a tell?"

I tossed her the ball and she ran up for a layup, but she misjudged the distance and the ball bounced off the rim.

I caught the rebound and lined up my jump shot. "It's something you always do that lets me know what you're planning." I released the ball, and it arched through the air and into the basket. "Swish!" I bragged. "That's more like it. Nothing but net."

"Well, what is it?"

"You always look where you're going to go."

"Doesn't everybody?" Melina said, looking confused. "How else am I supposed to see where I'm going?"

We both laughed, and I ran over to get the ball. "I can show you a few tricks to make it harder for people to see it."

"That'd be great. I *really* want to make starting lineup this year."

"Stick with me and you'll make it for sure," I said, tossing the ball back and forth between my hands. "I'll even help you fix that layup."

Melina bent down and retied her laces. "We can't all

be superstars, Taylor. Are you ready for tryouts Monday?"

"I've never been more ready. We're definitely going to beat the Ravens in the playoffs this year."

"You think so?" she said, sounding surprised.

"I know so. And I'm going to win the tournament MVP."

The Most Valuable Player award went to the playoff tournament's best basketball player. My older brother, Jason, won it two years in a row when he went to Central.

"I don't know," she said, clearly unimpressed with my swagger.

"MVP goes to the person who scores the most points. And I'm definitely going to score the most points." I took another shot. It wasn't pretty, but it went in.

Melina caught the ball as it fell. "It's a team sport, you know. It's not all about you."

But I snatched it out of her hands. "When I see the shot"—I lifted the ball above my head—"I take it." I threw the ball, but missed.

"That's for sure." She rolled her eyes.

"To win MVP, I've got to be the best!" I said, dribbling the ball back and forth between my legs.

Melina sighed. "It's getting dark. I'm going to head home."

"I want to keep playing," I said. "Just for a little bit longer."

"All right."

Her voice sounded different, almost sad, and I felt bad for showing off so much. "See you tomorrow morning?"

"Maybe," she said, and turned and walked away.

Maybe? What'd she mean by that? But I shrugged it off and continued playing.

I misjudged my next shot and had to chase the ball down the court. But when I picked it up, the strange sensation hit me again. It felt like I was being watched.

I scanned the area and noticed the silhouette of a person behind the big cypress tree. It was a girl. As I moved toward her, she turned and ran off, so I wasn't able to get a good look at her. But she was about my height, with big, bushy hair.

Who was she? And why was she watching me from the shadows? Did I know her?

Then it hit me. The Ravens! There was a girl with big, bushy hair on their basketball team.

She was probably a spy, sent to check out the competition.

The Western Ravens were the defending division

champions. They were also the Central Tigers' greatest rivals. Both schools took basketball very seriously, and both teams played to win. But that was where the similarities ended.

The Ravens played dirty. And everybody knew it.

I wouldn't go so far as to say they cheated, but they definitely bent the rules. If the refs weren't looking, you could count on a Ravens player to pinch, trip, or even hip-check their opponents.

If Coach Carter ever caught a player on our team trying something like that, he'd have them warming the bench for the rest of the game. But the Ravens' coach encouraged the bad behavior.

Unfairly or not, the Tigers had lost every game to the Ravens for as long as I could remember. But all that was going to change this year. This year was going to be different.

"Hey, Raven! You spying on us now?" I called after her.

No answer. She was long gone.

It didn't matter. I figured the next time we saw each other would be on the court—and I'd let my skills do the talking.

2

THE BIG DAY

A loud pounding on my bedroom door woke me early Monday morning.

"Time to get up, Taylor!" Mom called out. "Today's the big day."

"I'm up!" I yelled back. "I'm up."

The thought of going to school would usually put me in a lousy mood, but not today. Nothing was going to ruin this feeling. Today, school meant basketball.

I hopped out of bed and glanced around my tiny room. Like with school, I had a love-hate relationship with it. I loved all the fun times I'd had here, but I hated how small it was. My parents called it "cozy," but it could barely fit my stuff. And there wasn't much, just a captain's bed and a small desk set. In fact, it was so small, I had to put my dresser inside my closet.

Each year I got bigger and my room got smaller.

I glanced at the posters on the walls. On one was the outline of a girl making a layup, filled with splattered, bright-colored paint. The other was a picture of the Harlem Globetrotters. Mom and Dad took me and Jason to see them last year.

There was also a pennant from the UCLA Bruins, my favorite team, and a Nerf hoop strategically stuck to the wall above my clothes hamper. Nothing made it into the wash without going through the hoop first.

Basketball was my life. Obviously.

Case in point. My first basketball experience.

I'd only been three years old, so I didn't actually remember it myself. But I'd heard the story so many times I could tell it in my sleep. My parents—especially my dad—told it to anyone who would listen.

The whole family had been sitting together in the living room. Jason was eight and had one of those little foam basketball hoop toys with the suction cup. He'd stuck it to a wall and everyone was taking turns trying to make a basket.

Even though I could barely walk, I grabbed the ball and tossed it at the hoop, and it sailed through the air and landed right inside. The shot was a total fluke, but Mom and Dad had cheered and danced around—even

Jason had joined in—and from that day forward, I was hooked.

That was the story anyway, and my parents, especially Dad, were sticking to it. I didn't even know if it was really true or not.

The few times I'd questioned it, my parents had just shown me old photos taken at various ages and locations as proof. Photos where I stood proudly holding a basketball, smiling back at the camera. But there were pictures of Jason doing the same thing. In fact, there were even pictures of both of us fighting over the ball.

Jason used to love basketball as much as I did, maybe even more. We'd played together ever since I could walk, but he was way better than me and almost always kicked my butt in one-on-one. Lately, though, things were different. Basketball was just another annoyance for him. And so was I.

"TOES!" Jason yelled, grinning in the open doorway.

Toes was his nickname for me. Because I went through a lot of sneakers and always wore them out at the big toe. Jason thought it was hilarious. I hated it.

Mainly because it was a reminder that new sneakers were expensive and we couldn't afford them. Sometimes I had to play for weeks with busted shoes.

I rolled my eyes. "What?"

"Remember what I told you!"

"What's that?" I asked, feigning ignorance.

"Take the shot!" he said. "Always take the shot!"

"Okay, *Mom*."

Jason snorted and walked away. I hated when he called me Toes, he hated when I called him Mom. It drove him absolutely crazy. So naturally I said it any time I could. It was one of my life's greatest pleasures.

After I got dressed, I picked up the dirty clothes lying around the bedroom floor, and one by one, tossed them through the hoop above the hamper. Then I ran downstairs, excited to see Dad and talk to him about basketball tryouts.

Dad played guitar in a rock band called Teddy and the Players, and one of their new songs had made it onto the radio. They were going on tour. We were used to Dad being away with the band on weekends, but this time it was going to be for over a month.

I missed him when he was away. We all did. Especially Mom.

But if he wasn't playing gigs, he wasn't making any money. And we really needed the money. Mom and Dad never said anything to us directly, but I'd overheard them arguing about it plenty of times.

Mom wanted Dad to get a regular, steady job, but he was dedicated to the band. The only thing my dad liked more than basketball—besides our family, of course—was music.

I was excited for him, even if it meant him going away. He was excited for me to play basketball.

I got dressed quickly and raced to home base. That's what my parents called the kitchen. If they weren't watching TV, you could almost always find them in the kitchen.

Mom was trying to get my little sister to eat her breakfast—Baby Gemma, as we all liked to call her. The new kid in town. She'd just turned eighteen months old and took up most of Mom's time and attention. It was a tough adjustment at first—I was used to being the baby of the house. Not anymore. Now, I was the dreaded middle child. Yuck.

I loved Baby Gemma. We all did. But truth be told, Mom and Dad hadn't planned on having another baby. They could barely afford to feed me and Jason. I'd overheard more than a few arguments about it leading up to the birth, but once Baby Gemma arrived, all that talk disappeared. Mostly.

Mom looked up and smiled. "Morning, sweetheart." She kissed me on the forehead as I grabbed a piece of jam toast off Baby Gemma's plate. "Have some breakfast. You need your strength this morning."

"That's right," Dad said, putting his coffee cup down

on the table. "You ready to show them how to play some basketball?"

I ran over and gave him a big bear hug, and he lifted me right up off the ground.

Jason was always getting in trouble, so he still got plenty of attention. He might not have wanted it, but he still got it. But as the middle child, I was used to being overlooked. So I was enjoying getting some attention for once. Unfortunately, Jason made sure it didn't last long.

"Yeah, right," he said. "It's only *girls'* basketball. It's not the same thing."

"Jason!" Mom snapped. "Stop that right now."

I liked to pretend his insults didn't hurt me, but that one always did. I stuck my tongue out at him. "You're just jealous because you can't play."

"HA!" Jason said, glaring at me.

Jason wasn't allowed to play basketball at his high school this year because he'd gotten into a bunch of fights last year. Even with his own teammates. On and off the court.

The school had given him plenty of warnings, but nothing worked. He couldn't control his anger and got into another big fight during the playoffs. So he was kicked off the team for a whole season.

Sure, I felt bad for him, but I also felt a little excited.

This year I'd be the only one playing basketball, so I'd get all the attention. "Basketball is my game now."

Jason scowled at me. "Yeah, right. Basketball will always be *my* game."

"Not today," I said smugly.

Jason started yelling, Baby Gemma started crying, and Mom and Dad tried to make peace. It was a typical morning in our house.

I grabbed my stuff and started for the door. I wasn't going to get pulled into another family fight. Not today. I wasn't going to let anything ruin this for me.

"You need to walk Poppy before you go," Mom called after me.

"But, Mom! I can't be late for tryouts."

"Then you'd better hurry," said Dad. "We've got to clean up here and take Baby Gemma to the doctor."

"Why can't Jason do it?"

"*I'm* not doing it," Jason said, running out of the kitchen and stomping up the stairs to his bedroom.

Dad gave me his best "do it for me" look. "Please?"

I let out an exasperated sigh, then ran over to the front entrance and grabbed my sneakers. In a split second, Poppy was standing in front of me wagging his tail.

As I pulled on my right sneaker, I noticed a strange

but familiar sensation. I looked down, and sure enough, the tip of my big toe was poking out of a tiny hole in the mesh.

Great. Just great.

3

ENEMY AMONG US

Melina was about to ring our doorbell when Poppy and I came racing around the block. The walk was probably too short, but it would have to do. I let him in the house and promised to make it up to him with a longer walk after school.

Melina and I were dressed almost exactly the same, in gray hoodies and black gym shorts. And we both wore tight ponytails for basketball. The only difference between us, besides our height, was our hair color— mine was blonde and Melina's was chestnut brown. Well, that and our sneakers, of course. Melina always wore nice *new* sneakers. Thankfully, she never commented on mine. She was great that way.

As we walked to school, we talked about basketball tryouts. Having both made the team last year, we were pretty confident we'd make this year's team. Especially since not that many girls tried out.

Summer vacation was barely over, but the days were already getting shorter. The air was cool and quiet, and when we cut across the soccer field toward the school, I noticed the grass still had dew on it.

Central Elementary looked like something from a scary movie. Old red bricks. Windows with protective wire cages. Peeling paint. The only thing that gave away it was a school was the large message board at the main entrance.

The board usually had encouraging quotes written on it. Today, in black letters, it said:

Join the Tigers!

Girls' basketball tryouts today.

Gymnasium at 8 a.m.

They may have called it tryouts, but pretty much anyone who showed up made the team. Last year, which was the first year Melina and I played, there were only twelve players on the team.

The outside doors to the school gymnasium were propped open and Coach Carter was standing nearby. He smiled and waved us over. "Welcome back, girls. Nice to see you again."

Coach Carter used to teach fifth grade, but was now our sixth-grade homeroom teacher. He was short, bald, and told really bad jokes. And he was always quoting famous people. He was okay as a teacher, but he was a great coach. At least, I thought he was. He really knew the game and its history.

"Go get yourselves warmed up," he continued. "I'll join you shortly."

We walked inside and I took a deep inhale through my nose. The familiar scent made my stomach tingle. It was a weird smell, like window cleaner and stinky socks, but there was nothing else quite like it.

Personally, I loved it.

Melina and I greeted the other girls. There were only ten of us so far, and I recognized them all, even the fifth graders.

The starting team roster was always made up of the best players on the team. Besides me, all of the girls from last year's starting lineup had moved on to middle school, but if I had to guess, this year's starters would be me, Siarra, Melina, Emma, and Zoe. The reserves, which was basically a nice way of saying the bench warmers, would be Lola, Natalie, Pari, Sarah, and Sophie.

Coach Carter came in with a new girl trailing shyly behind him. She was tall and fit and had big, bushy brown hair. I didn't recognize her at first, but when the shrill sound of Coach's whistle filled the gymnasium, the realization hit me like a punch to the gut.

It was her! The girl who had spied on me from behind the tree.

You've got to be kidding me.

I just stared at her, completely shocked, while the other players hustled over to the benches.

Coach noticed me standing there. "Taylor, let's go! Where's your hustle?"

I shook off my confusion and ran over to join the others.

The bench was an interesting place. A lot happened there during the course of the season. For the starting players, your spot on the bench became like your rank on the team. The pecking order. The closer you sat to the coach, the higher your rank.

I was the strongest player last year and earned my spot sitting right next to Coach Carter. I assumed this year would be the same. Siarra would probably end up sitting next to me, and Melina would be next to her, and so on. Players each had their place along the line.

"This is Nicole," Coach said, motioning to the new girl. "She's an excellent basketball player, and I'm excited for her to join our team."

Nicole smiled shyly and gave us an awkward wave,

then brought one hand to her neck and fidgeted with a thin gold necklace.

"Taylor, slide over and let Nicole have a seat."

I couldn't believe my ears. Slide over? What was Coach talking about? This was my spot. I'd earned it.

"Taylor?" Coach motioned with his hands as he repeated himself. "Slide over..."

I grumbled and made room for Nicole to sit down next to me.

I couldn't believe it. There was an enemy among us. "What are you doing here?" I asked. "Don't you play for the Ravens?"

The girls oohed and aahed at the revelation. This was big news, and they immediately started asking Nicole questions.

"Did you really play for the Ravens?" Melina asked.

"How many kids go to Western?" Emma asked.

Then Sarah chimed in from the far end of the bench. "Does Western have a pool in the basement?"

Nicole remained calm and answered each question. "Yes," she said, nodding to Melina. "I used to play for the Ravens." She looked at Emma. "I'm not sure how many kids go to Western. But it's bigger than Central. And, no," she said, looking down the bench to Sarah and giggling. "There's no pool."

"We've never beat the Ravens," Emma blurted out.

Even though it was true, I felt the need to defend our team's honor. "But this year is going to be different. Right, Coach?"

I looked over at Coach Carter. He was completely preoccupied with something on his clipboard.

"Right, Coach?" I repeated, louder.

He looked up from his clipboard and gave us a confused look. "What?"

"The Tigers are going to beat the Ravens this year!" I looked at my nearest teammates for support. A few heads nodded in agreement.

"Maybe I can help you beat them," Nicole said hopefully.

"Listen up!" Coach said, and blew his whistle. "We're not going to beat anyone by sitting around. Let's warm up." He walked to the center of the gym, and we all lined up in front of him.

Coach explained how much he loved "creating efficiencies"—an expression I remembered from last year —which meant he'd be using our warm-up time not only to get us in better shape but to share information about basketball.

As we stretched, he told us about practice times. Every Tuesday and Thursday at eight in the morning.

And a long series of core exercises (crunches, planks, and leg lifts) gave Coach enough time to go over the basic rules of the game: Five players per team on the court. Score more than your opponent to win. Score within the shot clock. Dribble the ball to advance. Offense must move the ball forward. Defenders could block or steal the ball. And so on.

Once everyone was clutching their stomachs in agony, he made us switch to jumping jacks. That's when we heard about the different player positions: point guard, shooting guard, small forward, power forward, and center.

We finished with deep knee bends while Coach told us about the number of games in the season and the end-of-season tournament, and then he ended the warm-up and asked everyone to jog two laps around the gym.

"Later," I said to Melina, then sprinted as fast as I could. On my second time around, I even lapped some of the slower kids.

I was the first player finished and joined Coach Carter at center court. "Good hustle, Taylor," he said. I was exhausted and had to bend over to catch my breath.

Nicole strode in right behind me, barely breathing hard. *Figures.*

"Hey," she said. "Looks like you've got a hole in your shoe."

Argh. I gave her a fake smile. "Thanks."

More players finished and joined us at center court. When Melina arrived, she strolled up next to me. "It's only tryouts and you're already the most competitive," she said, tsk-tsking me like I'd done something wrong.

"So what's wrong with that?"

"Nothing," Melina said under her breath as the stragglers trickled in.

I was about to ask what she meant, but Coach blew his whistle to get our attention.

He took basketballs off a large metal rack and tossed one to each player as he explained the next exercise. "The objective is to be the first player to make two baskets on each of the six hoops around the gym."

Once each player had a ball, he raised his hand. "On your marks. Get ready..." As soon as he dropped his hand and blew the whistle, everyone ran toward the nearest basket and started shooting.

Everyone except me.

The other players were suffering from mob mentality—where one person started doing something and everyone else followed suit. But the more kids at a hoop, the harder it would be to make two baskets.

Melina called out to me, but I ignored her and ran to a basket with no other players. Whatever she was mad about would have to wait.

I made an easy layup and snagged the ball before it

even hit the ground, then ran back to the free-throw line, sized up my shot, and made another basket. One down, five to go.

Most of the kids were still trying to score on the same crowded basket. Not me. As soon as I made my second shot, I bolted for the next open basket.

As I went from basket to basket, I watched the other players. Some kids were taking wild 3-point shots that missed by a mile and bounced across the gym. They lost precious time running after stray balls.

But I was strategic. I followed a pattern. Run up and make the easy layup, then make the second shot from the free-throw line. I needed to show Coach Carter and the other players that I was the best. This was a competition, and I had to win. Especially against Nicole.

I scanned the gym to find her, and just my luck, she was the only other player taking the competition seriously. But there was no way I would let her beat me. I turned up the heat and sprinted to the next basket.

From the corner of my eye, I watched her move through the next two hoops just as quickly as me. And although we'd started at different baskets, somehow we ended up right next to each other for the final one.

I ran in for a layup, but Nicole had already thrown her ball over my head and it snuck through the hoop a second before mine. We were tied. Next point won.

Nicole grabbed her ball and lined up her final shot.

I can't let her win. I just can't.

She took her shot and the ball floated through the air in a perfect arc. It was headed straight for the basket. I could tell it was going to go in.

Without even thinking, I thrust my ball straight at hers, and they collided in midair just above the basket, the momentum of my ball knocking hers completely off its trajectory. Her ball was sent hurtling away in the opposite direction, while mine landed nearby. *Success.*

I shrugged innocently. "Sorry."

"No worries," Nicole replied, then ran after her ball.

As I picked up mine, I noticed Melina staring at me from the next basket over. *Did she see what I did?*

Whatever. She was acting weird anyway. I turned away from her and focused on sinking my last basket. I took a deep breath and released. *Swish.* Nothing but net.

"Yes!" I yelled, and pumped a triumphant fist at my side.

I grabbed the ball and ran over to Coach Carter at the center of the gym. "I won!" I said, beaming. "I'm the first one to get two baskets in each hoop."

Coach blew his whistle and called everyone in. I felt a twinge of guilt, but it didn't last. I felt too good about how well I was doing. I'd shown everyone, especially Nicole, exactly what I was capable of.

To be honest, I'd even surprised myself with that stunt. But it had to be done. Losing wasn't an option.

I walked over and stood next to Melina, who was staring at me with a pout on her face. What was up with her lately?

"Great job out there, everyone," Coach said.

Emma's hand shot up. "Will everyone make the team?"

"Basketball is played with two teams of five players on the court. Our league allows a maximum of twelve players, five players on the court and seven players on the bench."

The newer players looked at each other, confused. After all, this was basketball not math.

Thankfully, Coach Carter quickly put them out of their misery. "Yes, everyone here is on the team."

We all cheered.

"Next practice is Thursday morning. I'll be assigning positions, so think about which one you want to play."

I didn't have to think about it at all. I had my plan all figured out—I'd be the starting shooting guard, I'd lead the team in points, and then I'd win the MVP award.

"Now, I have one more very important question to ask you," Coach said, with a serious look.

Everyone quieted and paid close attention.

"I need you to think about this question very

carefully."

Silence.

"Do you want to play to have fun, or do you want to play to win?"

More silence.

"If you want to play for fun," he continued, "everyone will receive equal playing time regardless of skill or merit. If you want to play to win, some of you may only receive a few minutes of court time per game."

Melina and I looked at each other and nodded.

"Raise your hand if you want to play to win," Coach Carter said.

My hand shot up immediately. Siarra, Melina, and Nicole's went up too. A few more followed and we had the majority. Eventually, the few kids that didn't have their hands up raised theirs as well.

It may not have been a very fair way to decide, but I certainly wasn't going to say anything. I was the best player on the team, so this meant I'd get even more game time.

Coach Carter smiled. "Looks like we'll be playing to win!"

"YES!" I cheered, unable to contain my excitement. My whole body felt energized. Everything was coming together.

This was going to be the best season ever.

4

CLASSROOM SURPRISE

After tryouts, Melina and I quickly changed into our regular clothes and headed for Coach Carter's classroom on the third floor.

"What do you think of Nicole?" I asked.

Melina shrugged. "She seems nice."

"She's definitely a good player," I said as we entered the classroom.

When I sat down, I noticed there was a new desk set up right next to mine.

"This is Nicole," Coach Carter said to the class, motioning to the all-too-familiar girl who stood by his side. "She's a new student at Central Elementary. She'll be joining our class, so I expect you all to say hello and help her feel welcome."

She waved shyly and gave an embarrassed smile. She couldn't seem to stop fidgeting with her necklace.

"Nicole, you can take the empty seat next to Taylor."

Nicole shuffled her way toward me and whispered, "Hi Taylor."

I smiled awkwardly. "Hi, Nicole."

As Melina, Siarra, and Mia—who all sat nearby—welcomed her brightly, I felt a twinge of guilt about what I did during practice. But I pushed it away. We all make mistakes. I wouldn't let it happen again.

Coach Carter pulled out a stack of papers from his desk drawer, then caught my eye. "Taylor, please distribute these for me?"

Ugh. I shouldn't have made eye contact. Rookie mistake.

I took the papers from him, then walked to the opposite side of the room and started handing them out.

Coach Carter glanced around the classroom. "Because we have a new student, we're going to start today off with an icebreaker. Taylor is handing out get-to-know-your-classmates bingo cards. Each square on the card contains a fact. Your job is to find a classmate who fulfills each square. You must ask another student the question, and if they say yes, you write their name in the square."

I quickly made my way through the room, saving

Nicole for last. I slid the bingo card onto her desk without making eye contact and took my seat.

"There are twenty-four students, and there are twenty-four bingo squares—plus the free center square. Is everybody ready?" he asked. "Remember, this is blackout bingo. You need to fill every square. You have fifteen minutes..." He waited until the room was completely silent, then shouted, "BEGIN!"

Instant chaos. Desks were jostled. Chairs were pushed. Students elbowed their way past one another in search of their friends.

Lucky for me, Melina sat right behind me. I turned around to face her. "Have you ever been to Disneyland?" I asked, knowing she had.

"Yes!" she replied. "Do you have a male sibling?" She scribbled my name in the square before I even answered.

I nodded and moved on to Siarra, who also sat nearby. She filled in my "youngest in the family" square. Siarra was an only child, so technically the youngest.

Even though Nicole seemed a little shy, it looked like she was having fun getting to know the other students. I saw an opening and moved over to her.

"Let's do this, Nicole." I looked down at the bingo card and read out questions in rapid-fire succession until I got a yes.

"Do you have a sister?"

"No."

"Do you have allergies?"

"No."

"Do you like math?"

"Yes! It's my favorite subject."

"Okay," I said. "Your turn. Fire away."

Nicole did the same thing to me until I answered "yes" to "Do you have a dog?"

"Oh, I love dogs," she said. "What's its name?"

"Poppy," I said. "But my brother calls him Poopy." We both laughed.

I had to admit, she seemed really nice. Now I felt even worse about my behavior earlier.

We both moved on to other students, but before I could complete my card, Jake Murphy yelled, "Bingo!" and we returned to our regularly scheduled subject. Math.

I wasn't great at math—it was my least favorite subject—but I still usually passed the tests. Unfortunately, we'd just started learning about integers and I was finding the concepts hard to understand.

After only a few minutes of the lesson, it was clear that Nicole didn't find integers hard. She raised her hand on every question. She obviously excelled in math *and* basketball and was the perfect student. *Perfect. Just perfect.*

As a not-so-perfect student, I found it hard to focus. Instead, I daydreamed about playing shooting guard and winning MVP for the rest of the class.

The recess bell rang just as a thought struck me —*What if Nicole wants to play shooting guard?*

I leaped up from my desk, turned to Melina, and said, "Hurry! I need to talk to you right away." I took her by the hand, and we ran for the door. We were the first students out of the classroom.

As soon we got outside, Melina asked, "What's wrong? Is everything okay?"

I realized I couldn't tell her what was really bothering me, because it didn't even make any sense. She would think I was freaking out about nothing.

So I blurted out the first horrible thought that came into to my mind. "My parents might be getting a divorce."

Divorce. Hearing the word out loud was like a punch in the gut.

Lately, things *had* been difficult between Mom and Dad. They were arguing even more than usual...

What if they *were* getting divorced?

5

PLAY TO WIN

It was only our second practice, but Coach Carter had us working hard.

First we worked on our ball handling skills, moving the ball around our bodies—between our legs, around our waists, even behind our heads. Then we practiced dribbling while passing the ball through our legs.

Next, Coach had us do layup lines, where a team splits into two groups behind the foul line, one on each side of the key. The first player on the left passes the ball to the first player on the right, who then goes up for the layup.

The next player on the passing side grabs the rebound and passes to the next kid in the layup line. Shooters move to the back of the passing line and passers move to the back of the layup line.

It was a fun drill, and it moved pretty fast.

Coach watched each player carefully and took notes on his clipboard, and after Nicole made her layup, he called her over to speak with him while I watched from the back of the line. He glanced up, noticed me looking at him, and nodded. Was he talking to her about me?

Nicole stayed next to him as I made my way up the line, and after I made my layup, he called me over.

"Taylor," he said, smiling. "Nicole is a strong shooting guard too. For games, I was thinking that you could each play fifty-fifty."

My stomach sank at the thought of sharing the position. My play time would be cut in half! I needed to score as many points during the season as possible to win MVP—and giving up half my playing time was *not* part of the plan.

I blurted out the first thing I thought might help my case. "I thought you said we were going to play to win!"

Coach Carter looked a little surprised, but nodded. "Well, what do you propose?"

"I don't know... maybe one-on-one? First player to score eleven points gets starting position."

He looked over at Nicole. "Are you okay with that?"

She nodded. "Sounds good."

"Okay," Coach said. "First player to eleven wins.

Baskets are a point each and you need to win by two. Nicole, you have possession."

Games start with something called a check, to make sure both teams—or players, in our case—are ready. Nicole took the ball, bounced it to me, and I bounced it back. The game was on.

Nicole was a real player. She knew the game, had great ball handling skills, and could shoot too. She moved in and made her first shot. It went right in.

This wasn't going to be easy. She was playing to win.

But so was I.

I slapped the ball away from her and gained possession, then dribbled around her, made a layup, and tied the game.

We were evenly matched in shooting and defense. It was like playing my shadow—if my shadow acted like a giant brick wall that anticipated my every move. Nicole put herself wherever I tried to be.

We traded baskets back and forth. She'd score a few baskets, then I'd gain possession and tie things up. I'd pull ahead for a basket or two, but she'd come right back.

Soon, we were tied at ten.

The other players had stopped doing layups and were watching our game.

I had possession. All I had to do was sink the next two baskets. I smiled to myself. *The game is mine.*

I tried my signature move, bouncing the ball through her legs, but Nicole was right there. She bumped me, stole the ball, and made an easy layup.

Now she was in the lead, and it was her ball. If she made the next shot, she'd win the game.

No way. Not today. And especially not in front of the whole team. No way was I going to lose this. I'd tied it up before and I could do it again.

I'd watched her play and could anticipate her moves perfectly. I could be a shadow too—I wouldn't let her escape me. She started for the right-hand side, faked left, and bolted hard to the right again.

I anticipated her move and moved to the right. But I lost my footing and went down. Hard.

Nicole made a run for the basket.

My heart pounded inside my chest, and I felt my face flush.

The whole world seemed to move in slow motion.

Everything went silent.

Nicole leaped up, extended her arms, and the ball left her hand. My eyes followed as it arched slowly through the air. It hit the backboard right in the middle of the square...

And went in.

The other players cheered and screamed, and my whole world came crashing back to reality.

The game was over. Our practice was over. My life was over.

I wasn't the best player on the team. I wasn't going to be shooting guard. And I definitely wasn't going to win MVP.

I closed my eyes, wishing I could just disappear. But unfortunately, when I opened them, I was still sitting on the floor like a loser. And the other players were all congratulating Nicole.

Melina came over and helped me up. "Are you okay?"

I thought about blaming everything on the hole in my shoe, but decided against it. I didn't know what else to say, though. I wasn't okay, but I had no one to blame but myself.

"Yeah." I sighed and brushed myself off. "I'm fine."

Nicole walked over to us. "Good game," she said, extending a hand.

I grumbled and reluctantly shook it.

"Look," she said. "I don't mind playing fifty-fifty during the games."

"Really?" I was shocked. She was willing to give up *half* her playing time? I felt like a complete jerk.

"Sure. No problem."

Coach interrupted us, and said, "I'm afraid that's not how things work."

"What do you mean?" I asked.

"You challenged Nicole and you lost. She gets to be the starting shooting guard. I'll work with you on another part of your game."

I shook my head in disbelief. This was my worst nightmare. My dream of winning MVP was over. "But Nicole said it was okay," I pleaded.

Coach shook his head.

"But Coach..."

"No buts, no buts, no coconuts," he said, dismissively. Coach used this silly phrase every time someone complained, but he'd never used it on me before. It really stung. But there was no use trying to argue. It was over.

"Listen up," he began. "This is our starting lineup. Nicole..."

I froze in anticipation, and a knot of pain erupted in my stomach.

"You're my starting shooting guard."

The blood drained from my face. I felt dizzy and light-headed.

"Taylor," he continued. "Point guard."

Ugh! I felt sick to my stomach. I clenched my fists

and stared at a spot on the floor, desperate to steady myself. *This can't be happening.*

Coach told everyone else their positions, but I barely heard him. I was still in shock.

I couldn't believe I'd lost. I couldn't believe I wasn't going to be shooting guard. I loved playing that position.

The shooting guard was usually the team's best shooter, and the position was perfect for me. My whole life was about taking the shot. I was good at it.

It was the *only* thing I was good at.

What was I supposed to do now?

6

PICKING ON POPPY

I stared vacantly at the wall of the sixth-grade classroom, then down at the floor, toward the door... anywhere but directly at Coach Carter.

He was teaching class as if nothing had happened. As if the world hadn't ended. As if he hadn't ruined my life.

I became angrier with each passing minute. And by the end of English class, my mind had completely transformed him. He went from Coach Carter, *greatest* coach on Earth, to Mister Carter, *worst* teacher in the world. Until finally, inside my head, I was calling him an old Turd Farter.

The rest of the morning passed in an angry red blur. I kept clenching and unclenching my fists. I wanted to destroy something. Actually, I wanted to destroy some*one*.

Someone who was sitting right next to me.

Nicole had also been acting like nothing happened. And, even though I knew it wasn't her fault, she was a constant and painful reminder of my situation. I wasn't going to play shooting guard, or score the most points, or win the MVP award at the tournament.

"It's ridiculous. She got lucky. If I hadn't slipped..."

Melina and I had finished our lunches and were walking around the schoolyard. I was still fuming about the whole situation.

"It was *really* close," she replied. "And she's really good."

This comment made me even angrier. "You think she's better than me?"

"No..." Melina looked frustrated. "I mean, I don't know."

I scowled. "Maybe I won't play at all. Let's see how far the team gets without me."

Melina stopped and grabbed my arm. "But the only reason I even joined the team was because you!" She crossed her arms over her chest. "You're not *seriously* thinking about quitting? For real?"

"No," I replied, shaking my head. "I'm not quitting. I'm just really upset."

"You'll beat her next time," she said, trying her best to console me.

But I was having none of it.

"What does it even matter? She's going to score all the points anyway. I've got no chance of winning MVP."

My voice sounded annoying. Whiny. It was like I was turning into a different person. I was usually positive, focused on the good things in life. But since losing my position as shooting guard, all I wanted to do was complain.

In the kitchen later that night, I told Mom what happened.

I poured out my guts to her. I told her everything. How bad I felt. How unfair it all was. How all my plans were falling apart. How, basically, my life was over.

And, somehow, Mom turned it into a lecture about me not helping out enough.

"I'm sorry you won't get to play the position you wanted," she said. "Change is hard, but maybe it's a good thing. Some things need to change around here too. With Dad being away longer, you and Jason need to step up and help out more."

"What does that have to do with anything?" I demanded.

"We're a family," she continued. "We help each other out. And right now, I need you to walk the dog."

"Thanks, Mom," I muttered as I grabbed Poppy's leash. "I feel much better now."

"And if you see Jason," Mom said, "tell him I need to speak with him."

I walked Poppy around the block, sulking the whole time, and when I passed by the school, I noticed Jason sitting on the steps.

"Mom's looking for you," I said.

"Yeah. That's why I'm here." He leaned down to pet Poppy. "Dumb dog."

"Don't say that. It's mean. Poppy's a great dog."

"I'm just kidding," he said. "Poopy *is* great dog. Aren't you Poopy?"

"Very funny. Did you and Mom get in another fight?"

Jason immediately changed the subject. Now, instead of picking on Poppy, he turned his attention on me. "Damn, Toes! Those sneakers look rough!"

"I know," I said. "I've asked Mom for a new pair."

"How you gonna play ball in those? Or are you just gonna warm the bench this season?"

"No! I'm going to be point guard," I said, and immediately regretted it.

"Point guard?" He laughed. "You might as *well* be warming the bench!"

I tried to explain what happened, but it didn't help.

"You challenged her and you lost," Jason said, shaking his head. "What a loser!"

Anger welled up in me, and my face got hot.

I don't have to take this.

I pulled on Poppy's leash and started to walk away.

Jason knew he'd hurt me, and like a shark that smelled blood, he went in for the kill. "You're never gonna win MVP if you're not shooting guard!" he called out.

I continued walking, faster now, a fury building up inside me.

"You just gonna let them take it from you?" he yelled.

I spun around and faced him. "What am I supposed to do?"

"Whatever it takes!"

That was it. The pent-up anger and frustration inside me released all at once. "And get kicked out like you did!" I yelled. "You'd love that, wouldn't you? You're just jealous that I still get to play. I still have friends. You're the loser and everyone knows it!"

Jason's face sank. He'd hurt me and I had hurt him right back. I felt terrible, but I didn't want to wait around to see what would happen next.

I turned and sprinted away, Poppy following closely behind me. I ran and ran and didn't look back. I ran until I couldn't run anymore.

When I leaned over to catch my breath, Poppy jumped up and licked the salty tears from my face. I scooped him up in my arms and hugged him tightly.

Why was Jason such a jerk all the time? Did it make him feel good to make me feel bad? What a horrible way to be.

Then again... maybe he had a point. Maybe I needed to stop feeling sorry for myself and *do* something.

My old self was the best player on the team. My old self was shooting guard. My old self was determined to become MVP.

I needed to get back to being my old self.

And to do that, I needed to get my position back.

One way or another.

7

CHALLENGE ACCEPTED

I arrived at practice early, before any of the other players, to speak with Coach Carter in the gym office—a small room tucked against one side of the stage.

"I'm offering you something special," he said, holding up a blue wristband. "If you accept this, it means you'll be my floor captain."

I frowned. "You're just trying to make me feel better about not being shooting guard. Floor captain isn't even a real title."

"It's not an official league role," he admitted, leaning back against the desk and crossing his arms. "But you can make it real. And if you take it seriously, so will the team."

He seemed sincere, so maybe it *was* a real thing? I walked over to one of the trophy cases that lined the office walls. The MVP trophy was the largest award and towered over all the others. "Do I have to play point guard the *whole* season?"

"You don't learn new things over night," he said, coming to stand next to me at the trophy case. "It takes time and practice. As floor captain *and* point guard, you can have a huge influence on the team—even more than scoring points."

I read some of the names engraved on the MVP trophy. Jason's name was there twice, taunting me. "Yeah, right," I said, and rolled my eyes.

"Watch point guards like Magic Johnson, Steve Nash, and Stephen Curry," Coach continued, "and study how they play. The point guard is someone who sees potential. Who draws people out to be the best they can be. Who gives the pep talk or the kick in the pants."

He looked at me like he expected me to know what he was talking about. I didn't.

"What do you say, Taylor? Will you accept these new challenges?"

"Can I still play shooting guard for some games?" I asked hopefully. "If I want to win MVP, I need to score some points."

Coach sighed and shook his head. "You need to focus on helping the team get better, not winning MVP.

Besides, the MVP isn't always the person who scores the most points."

"What do you mean?"

"The best players understand that the team always comes first. They expect, and demand, the best from themselves and their teammates."

"I do demand the best," I said. "From everyone."

"The point of making you my floor captain and point guard is for you to help me create the strongest team. It's not about scoring the most points, it's not even about winning—it's about helping each member of the team be their best. Nicole is an excellent shooter. But she doesn't know the game as well as you do. You're a much more well-rounded player."

Coach went on, but the only thing that stuck with me was "She doesn't know the game as well as you do." The words kept repeating inside my head.

When he finished, he placed the wristband on the desk. "Wear it or don't wear it. It's up to you." He started for the door. "Practice is about to start."

After he left, the room was eerily quiet. I picked up the wristband from the desk and examined it from every angle. Did I want to focus on helping the team, or did I want to score the most points and win MVP?

The answer was obvious—I wanted to score points

and win MVP. Unfortunately, that wasn't the answer Coach was looking for.

But... maybe there was a way to do both?

If I took this opportunity, I'd be in charge of the whole team. I'd get to make all the decisions. I'd be in charge of the plays. Essentially, I'd be Nicole's boss.

She'd have to do whatever I told her to.

I pulled on the wristband and sprinted out to the gym. "Make way!" I hollered, and ran onto the court. "Floor captain coming through. New floor captain coming through!"

Melina was the first to congratulate me, and the other players followed. They all gathered round to pat me on the back or shake my hand.

I looked Nicole square in the eyes as I shook her hand.

"I've got big plans for us," I said, then gave her a big smile.

8

CHELSEY

After everyone finished congratulating me, Coach Carter had us all line up. A young woman I'd never seen before was standing next to Coach Carter. She was tall and fit with shoulder-length blonde hair, and she was wearing a UCLA Bruins outfit.

"We have a very special guest today," he said. "This is Chelsey. She played for the Tigers when she went to school here, and now she plays for the UCLA Bruins. She's this year's end-of-season tournament ambassador."

Everyone oohed and aahed, and Chelsey smiled and waved at us.

"Hi, everybody," she said. "It's nice to meet you."

I expected her to give a typical Coach Carter pep talk. You know, a boring speech about doing your best and giving every game 110 percent. Only she didn't do that.

"Coach Carter asked me to tell you what I love about basketball. And the funny thing is, what I love most isn't really about the game at all. It's not about championships, making the perfect jump shot, or scoring the winning basket just before the buzzer goes off. Those things are all great, but the thing I love most about basketball is the friendships."

This was definitely not the speech I was expecting.

She told us all about her time at Central, playing in different leagues, and playing at the college level. This was her first year as an ambassador. Basically, she went around to different schools and talked about basketball.

"Take a look at the girls sitting around you," she said, encouraging us to do this with her hands.

Heads turned left and right as we all quickly looked at each other. Melina and I shared a smile when our eyes met.

"If they're not already, these girls are going to become your best friends. Not just teammates. Not just good friends. *Best* friends."

She told a few funny stories—she was a really good storyteller—and we all hung on her every word. It meant a lot that they were coming from someone who used to be where we were now.

"Best friends are the people who will be there for you when you need them most. The ones you know you can always count on. They'll be there to cheer you on in good times and give you a shoulder to cry on in bad ones."

I glanced around and saw Siarra listening intently. And she wasn't the only one. Chelsey's talk about friendship was having a big effect on the whole team—including me.

"I'm still best friends with my teammates from years ago," Chelsey continued. "And even with those friends I don't see every day, when we run into each other at weddings and special occasions, it's like no time has passed at all. We hug and we're immediately transported back in time. We're joking around as if we're sitting on the bleachers waiting for our next game to start. Only nowadays we don't braid each other's hair like we used to."

She paused, allowing us to take in her words, before announcing, "This year, the tournament will be hosted by the Ravens at Western Elementary."

Nicole's whole body slumped at this news and her hand immediately went to her necklace.

"Each team plays four games during the regular season," Chelsey continued. "If you lose two games you're out. If you only lose one game, you make the Tournament."

Chelsey answered some of our questions, then said she'd be keeping an eye on us and hoped she would see us at the tournament.

We didn't make the tournament last year, but we'd make it this year. We just had to. It felt like I'd been waiting for this tournament my whole life.

9

FULL-COURT PRESS

It was the same school, the same gym, the same Coach —even the same players—but everything was somehow changed. Nothing was going the way it was supposed to. Nothing felt right.

Nicole was in my old spot on the bench. My old sneakers were too small and felt tight—the mesh had completely given way on the right shoe and my big toe poked out of the hole like a turtle. My uniform was too big and felt awkward. Plus, the waistband wasn't tight enough, so I was constantly pulling my shorts up.

Over the past two weeks, Coach Carter had worked with every player on the team to try to help them learn their role. Hustle was rewarded. Laziness was punished. He didn't get upset if a player missed a shot or made a mistake, but if he thought you were slacking off, he'd make you run laps and threaten to bench you during games.

I didn't understand my new role at all. Nothing was clicking. I was used to getting set up to score points, not setting others up. We practiced plays like give-and-go, pick-and-roll, high post/low post, baseline out-of-bounds, and backdoor maneuvers, but in my new position as point guard, I was lousy at all of them.

We were running some typical practice drills when Coach pulled me aside.

"Do you understand the plays?"

"No," I replied. "And I suck as a point guard."

He laughed. "I know. But that's okay. You need to get comfortable being bad. It's an opportunity to learn, to get even better."

"But I don't get it," I said. "I'm a shooter. Why wouldn't you want me to score points?"

"You're more than just a shooter, Taylor. That's what I'm trying to teach you. The team needs you to work on all of your skills."

I scowled. "It doesn't make any sense."

"As point guard and team captain," he explained patiently, "you'll be my floor general. That means you'll be my eyes and ears on the court. You'll lead the offense, call out the plays, and set your teammates up for success. You'll help settle people down when the other team makes a run."

Then Coach went over the plays I was having trouble with. He explained where I was supposed to be on the court and what I was supposed to be looking for.

When he was finished, I glanced around and saw Nicole and Melina working together. Talking and laughing.

My stomach twisted and my cheeks flushed. First, Nicole stole my position on the team, and now she was working on my best friend.

My whole life was falling apart.

I had to show Coach Carter and the rest of the team that I was still the best. And suddenly, I heard the two words that could make that possible.

"Full court!" Coach called.

Finally, after weeks of struggling as a point guard, I was going to get the chance to prove I was the better player and deserved to be shooting guard. This was my opportunity to make everything right again.

"We're only ten players today. Let's get some five-on-five going," Coach said, then divided everyone into two teams.

The first team was me, Melina, Emma, Natalie, and Zoe. Nicole was on the opposing team, along with Siarra, Pari, Sophie and Sarah.

Coach tipped the ball and soon the game was in full swing.

It was better to practice playing full court. We had to build up our cardio, get used to running. In basketball, especially during games, you ran a lot.

Pari grabbed the ball and dribbled her way down the court. I wasn't her defender, but I went after her anyway. She was an okay player and handled the ball well, but she was no match for me—I was taller and faster, and my defense was as good as my offense.

My long arms and legs gave me the advantage as I forced her to her weak left side. She got flustered and took her eye off the ball, which hit her foot and rolled away.

I bolted past her and scooped it up, then scanned the court for the opposing players.

Sophie stood in front of me, but she posed no threat. She was a really nice girl but a terrible basketball player. She was slow and uncoordinated and was constantly tripping over her own feet.

I casually dribbled the ball back and forth between hands as I planned my next move. Then, in a flash, I faked right and made a hard left. Sophie tried to follow me, but lost her footing and fell.

I probably should have stopped and checked on her,

but I didn't. I just continued down the court with one objective. Put the ball in the hoop.

The other players didn't stand a chance against me. They were playing for fun, while I was playing to win. Just like my brother had taught me.

"Taylor!" Melina called. She was open and inside the key. But I saw a small opening for myself and took it, bolting toward the hoop and scoring an easy layup.

Melina gave me a look. "Try giving the rest of us a chance." It sounded friendly, but I could tell there was something more behind it.

I walked back across the court and grinned at her. "When I see a shot, I take it."

For the next few minutes, I continued to dominate. Almost every time I got the ball, I penetrated their team's defense, took the shot, and scored. Nicole played well, but she wasn't as determined as me.

I darted around the other kids and easily moved the ball up and down the court. All my opponents were left in the dust. No one could stop me. The ball was like an extension of my body.

Layup. *Yes.* Another two points.

It felt like I was getting more of my old life back with every point. Soon everyone, especially Coach Carter, would see exactly what I could do. He'd realize his mistake and give me back my position as shooting guard.

After making another basket, I sprinted back to help our defense. The best players never walked on the court during a game, they always ran. And I was definitely the best player.

The other team had possession, and Nicole got the ball. I moved in to cover her. She tried to dribble around me, but I completely shut her down.

"That's not going to do it," I said, trying to shake her confidence with trash talk. "What's the matter, Nicole? Afraid to play somebody with skills?"

Nicole's friendly smile disappeared. Honestly, she looked like she'd seen a ghost.

When she dropped her eyes, I saw my chance to show everyone who was the best. I slapped the ball away from her, jumped past her and took possession, then sprinted toward the basket.

"Later!" I called back as I ran down the court.

Nice burn, I congratulated myself. *That'll show her.* Nicole might have beaten me in that stupid contest, but I was back on top. I had the ball and was about to score. Everything was right in the world again.

I took long, casual strides toward the hoop and got ready for another easy layup. When I reached the basket, I jumped high into the air, my whole body stretching out.

But as I released the ball, a shadow fell over me. I wasn't alone.

THWAP!

A big open hand had swung past me and swatted the ball out of the air.

Nicole.

Not only had she managed to catch up to me and block my shot, now she had the ball and was sprinting toward *my* basket.

I chased after her, but it was too late. I couldn't catch her.

I watched as she darted around the other players like they were standing still, as she faked out her final opponent and made the easy layup. And it wasn't the last time either. In fact, for the next few minutes, Nicole's team completely dominated the game. They were like a finely tuned machine, everyone working together. They even used some of the plays that Coach had us working on.

Nicole had my number. She'd figured out my weakness and used it to her team's advantage. Every time I got the ball, Nicole was on me. I couldn't lose her.

Her team got the ball and made another run for our

basket. Nicole passed the ball to Siarra, who passed it to Sophie.

She scored.

Seriously?

This couldn't be happening. I was the best. I had always been the best. How could Nicole be better than me? What would the other players think of me? And Coach Carter?

My whole body slumped and I let out a strange sound, like a balloon slowly deflating.

I was never getting my old position back.

A FRIENDLY SURPRISE

After breakfast on Saturday morning, Mom took Baby Gemma and me to pick up a few things at the mall.

We were walking down the corridor, staring absent-mindedly in all the display windows, when we reached a popular sportswear store. My eyes opened wide as I noticed some awesome sneakers.

I'd been begging for a pair like these for months, but it couldn't hurt to try again.

"I really need a new pair of sneakers, Mom," I said, looking longingly in the window. "Mine are falling apart."

Mom glanced at the price and shook her head. "These are too expensive, honey. We'll find you a nice pair somewhere else."

I rolled my eyes. "You mean a *cheaper* pair."

"You know money is tight right now, Taylor. We've all got to make some sacrifices."

"It's okay," I said curtly. "I should've known better."

She sighed. "Now, don't be like that. You know we would if we could."

"Yeah, right."

"What's that supposed to mean?" she asked.

"Nothing..."

"No." She stopped and looked at me. "Tell me what's going on. You haven't been yourself at all lately."

"You wouldn't understand," I said.

"What do you mean?"

I must have been bottling up a lot of things because all of a sudden a flood of emotions came rushing out of me.

"You and Dad are always worrying about Jason or dealing with Baby Gemma," I said, my voice rising. "It's like I'm invisible."

"Invisible? Really?"

"Jason's always in trouble. Baby Gemma always needs something. I'm just the invisible middle kid. Nobody's got any time left over for me. Nobody cares what I'm going through."

Mom's face sank. She looked really sad. "Gemma is a baby. And Jason... well, Jason is hurting right now. He

made some bad choices and he's dealing with the consequences."

"What consequences?" I said. "He never gets in
trouble."

"That's not true."

I scowled. "My whole life is falling apart, and no one
cares."

"We do care. I'm sorry you don't get to play shooting
guard, honey. I know you're disappointed—"

"*Disappointed?* You just don't get it."

"But you still get to play..."

"But I'll never win MVP!" I was getting more and
more agitated.

"What's so important about winning MVP?"

"It means I'm the best!" I was shouting now. "It
means there's nobody better than me."

Mom shook her head. She obviously didn't get it. I'm
not sure why, but this made me so angry I lashed out
at her.

"You wouldn't understand because you've never
been the best at *anything*!"

If I thought Mom looked disappointed before, it was
nothing compared to her face when I said *that*. It was as
if I'd knocked all the wind out of her.

"I guess you and Jason are more alike than I
thought." She turned away from me and started to push

the stroller toward the exit. "Maybe Coach Carter made the right decision."

"What?" I was shocked. "How can you say that?"

"A family is a lot like a team, Taylor. They both need to work together and help each other out. I don't see a lot of that coming from you lately."

"What about Jason? He never helps out. He never does anything."

"And does he seem happy to you?" She sighed. "Failing out of school, kicked off the basketball team, and fighting with everyone... Do you really want to follow his example right now?"

I shook my head. "No, but..."

I walked behind her in silence. I couldn't believe I was the one getting in trouble. Again.

Suddenly, Mom stopped. "You know what, Taylor? You're right. I don't understand."

I had no idea what she was talking about.

"You get to play basketball with your friends. Coach Carter even asked you to be captain."

"It's not like winning MVP," I said. "Being captain doesn't mean anything."

"It *could* mean something," she said, pushing the stroller forward again.

Neither of us said anything else for a while.

Mom went into a clothing shop, and I stayed outside

with Baby Gemma. Suddenly, in the distance, I saw a familiar silhouette with big, bushy hair. It had to be Nicole. In a panic, I pushed the stroller inside the front of the store and hid, then peered around the corner to confirm it was Nicole. It was.

And she was with Melina.

Laughing and giggling, they strolled in my direction. They didn't go into any of the shops, they just kept coming. Getting closer and closer.

I ducked back inside and pushed my back up against the store wall. I didn't want to see them. And I definitely didn't want them to see me.

I looked up at the ceiling. What were they doing here? Together. Were they friends outside of school now too? This couldn't be happening. First basketball and now this.

Soon, they'd be walking right by the store. I took a deep breath and held it. Should I confront them? Should I tell them I know exactly what's going on?

Staying as flat against the wall as possible, I peeked over at the entrance and watched them walk past.

"Hey!" a voice called out.

"Ahh!" I spun around, feeling like my heart just leaped out of my chest.

I'd been so focused on not being seen by Nicole and Melina, I hadn't noticed my mom coming up behind me.

"What were you doing?" she asked.

"Nothing," I said, trying to regain my composure. "I was waiting for you."

"I'm all finished here. Let's go check out the other shoe store."

"I just want to go home," I said.

"Come on, you can at least give it a try. They might have something you like."

After seeing Melina with Nicole, I felt sick to my stomach and wanted to get as far away from everyone as possible. "I'm tired. Can I please just go home?"

Mom gave me a concerned look, but Baby Gemma started fussing.

"Fine," said Mom with an exasperated sigh. "Go ahead. But take Poppy out for his walk when you get home, okay?"

"No problem. I will."

Mom leaned in to give me a hug, but I turned and walked away from her. It was a jerk thing to do, but I couldn't help it. I was upset. There was no time to explain myself, and even if I wanted to, I don't think I could have.

What was I feeling? Anger? Sadness? Jealousy? There was a dangerous mixture of emotions rising up inside me, bubbling to the surface, ready to make me explode.

I darted toward the nearest exit and never looked back. I needed to get out of here. Fast.

Light-headed and breathing heavy, I pushed my way through the exit and made it outside. What was happening to me? Within minutes, I'd gone from angry, to upset, to sad. I felt emotionally overwhelmed, like I was losing control of myself.

I took a deep breath and started walking. My body was tense and needed to release some of its pent-up energy, so the fast walk quickly turned into a jog, and soon I found myself sprinting for home.

The familiar neighborhood surroundings flew by me as I ran flat out, past houses and apartments and parked cars. Past kids playing on front lawns and trees in the park. All the way to Central Elementary. It was like a giant magnet pulling me in.

Exhausted and completely out of breath, I stopped in front of the basketball court near the main school entrance and bent over, my hands on my knees. My lungs ached so bad they felt like they were going to burst open from the inside.

Still breathing heavily, I looked up at the basketball hoop.

Why?

Why did being the best at this game matter so much to me?

11

THE MARSHMALLOW CHALLENGE

There was no denying it. Nicole was a thief.

She was taking everything away from me. My seat on the bench. My position as shooting guard. My dream of winning MVP.

Now she was trying to steal my friends too.

I glared at her every time she spoke with Melina, Siarra, or anyone else I knew in class.

I was so jealous of Nicole, everything she did annoyed me. I hated the way she dressed, how she talked, even her smile.

I knew this obsession with her wasn't healthy. I had to put Nicole out of my mind and focus on something else.

Unfortunately, Coach Carter's new assignment was making that impossible. It was something called the

Marshmallow Challenge, and he'd put Nicole on a team with me, Melina, and Siarra.

Argh! Nicole was intruding on every part of my life. I just couldn't get away from her—on the basketball court or in the classroom.

Coach Carter held up a large clear plastic bag as he explained the assignment. "Each team will work together and compete to build the tallest free-standing structure. You have only eighteen minutes to build it, and you can only use the items in the bag."

Each bag contained a pack of twenty spaghetti strands, one yard of tape, one yard of string, and a single marshmallow.

Melina could tell I was upset and tried to cheer me up. "Come on," she said, bumping me gently on the shoulder. "It's better than math."

"Yeah," said Siarra, pulling out the items and placing them on Nicole's desk. She made a duckface and held the spaghetti under her nose like a mustache. "It'll be lotsa fun!"

Coach Carter raised his voice over the buzz of everyone talking. "Push your desks together if you need a bigger space to work."

The room exploded in raucous screeches, clangs, and crashes as students slid chairs across the floor and pushed desks together. I spun my desk around to face

Melina's and Siarra and Nicole joined their desks with ours.

Coach Carter explained more of the rules. The marshmallow had to sit undamaged on the top of the structure. Altering the marshmallow in any way was cause for immediate disqualification. The actual structure itself had to stand firm on its own. It couldn't be propped up, held, or suspended from the ceiling.

"I'm not sure I get it," Melina said.

"We're supposed to make a building with this stuff and put the marshmallow on top," Nicole explained. "We use the spaghetti, tape, and string to design a structure that holds the marshmallow."

"And the tallest one wins," I added, maneuvering my way in front of Nicole. I wanted to show her that I was the leader of this group. Not her.

I'd show her. I'd show everybody.

I wanted to win. I *needed* to win. Because somehow, winning this challenge felt like it would help me get my life back on track.

"Let's make a pyramid, like the ones in Egypt," Nicole suggested. She made a triangle shape with her hands. "We can start with a triangle and build it up from there."

"No." I said, shooting her idea down immediately. I didn't even want her on my team—I certainly wasn't going to use one of her ideas. "Let's not rush into it. We should hear everyone's ideas first, then decide."

Melina held up the spaghetti. "Okay. What if we make a thick spaghetti bundle and tape it right to the desk?"

I poked a hole in her idea too. "Then it would only go one level high."

"But you could tape more spaghetti to the first bundle," Nicole offered.

I glared at her.

"Or not," she added weakly and took a step back.

"We could divide up the spaghetti and each build a square with little pieces of tape," Siarra suggested. "Then we could put them on top of each another."

We wasted a few minutes talking and playing around with the supplies. I asked a lot of questions and shot down a lot of ideas. I managed to find something wrong with everything.

I wanted to win. My teammates just wanted to get started. We were all getting frustrated.

"Let's just try a few things out and see what happens," Siarra said.

I beckoned them with my hands. "Okay, give me some more ideas. What else should we try?"

The classroom was noisy, chatter and laughter

coming from all around us. But no one was laughing in our group.

Coach Carter moved from group to group examining the structures. When he walked past our table, he looked at his stopwatch. "Ten minutes left."

"Whatever we do," Melina said. "We'd better hurry."

Siarra glanced around. "Yeah. Everyone is way ahead of us."

She was right. I needed to make a decision fast. Time was running out.

Time... watch... hourglass...

BOOM! It hit me.

I grabbed a handful of spaghetti strands. "We can tie the spaghetti at the center and twist them open like an hourglass." I twisted the pieces so they fanned open at the top and bottom. "See?" I said, holding it up. "Then we can stack them on top of each another."

Siarra shrugged, looking thoroughly unimpressed. "Sure. Why not?" She divided the spaghetti into four equal piles.

"Fine," Melina said. "Let's just try *something*." She grabbed a pile of spaghetti and twisted it in her hand to create an hourglass shape.

Nicole cut off a piece of string and helped Melina tie off her bundle. "Okay," she said. "But how are they going to sit on top of each other?"

"We can use the tape," I snapped.

Nicole cut off another piece of string and offered it to me.

"That's too much string. Cut it into shorter pieces."

Nicole dropped the string on the desk and placed the scissors next to it, a defeated look on her face. "Someone else do it."

"Don't worry, Nicole," said Siarra. "Who cares?" She snatched up the scissors and chopped the string into even longer strands. "We're taking this way too seriously."

"Some of us are," Melina said.

"What's that supposed to mean?" I asked, but Melina completely ignored my question. She wouldn't even look at me. Instead, she slowly bent down and picked up a fallen spaghetti strand.

Was she moving that slow on purpose? And what did Siarra mean when she said, "Who cares?" *I* cared. We *all* needed to care. What was wrong with everybody? Didn't they want to win?

"Five minutes left," Coach Carter said. This put me into even more of a panic.

Siarra set her spaghetti hourglass down in front of us. "This is about the best I can do with mine." It actually looked pretty good.

"Nice job, Siarra," I said, happy someone had listened to my directions. My plan might work after all.

"But, how are we going to stack them on top of each another?" she asked. "All the edges are so uneven."

It was true. When the spaghetti fanned out, the pieces were uneven and stuck out at different angles. It would be next to impossible to stack them.

"Let me see..." I tried to balance my hourglass on top of hers, but it was hopeless.

"It's impossible," Melina said, her tone flustered, like she just wanted to be done with the whole project.

Worried that everyone would blame me, I felt my cheeks flush red.

But Nicole jumped in. "Let's try putting some tape across the top of the spaghetti," she suggested. "We can make a platform."

Siarra tore off a piece of tape and handed it to me.

I tried frantically to create a platform using the tape, but the first piece got stuck to itself and I had to throw it away. The next piece managed to stick to the spaghetti but didn't make a stable platform. The clock was ticking, and I was panicking.

"Come on! Help me think of something."

Melina lifted her hands as if to say "I give up," then gave Siarra a knowing look. They both took a step back from me.

Nicole, however, stepped forward and tore off another piece of tape. "Maybe we can tape them to each other." She handed me the tape and held her hourglass on top of Siarra's.

I wrapped tape around the spaghetti while Nicole kept the two hourglasses steady. Melina and Siarra jumped back in and helped.

"It isn't pretty," Siarra said, taping the bottom pieces to the desk. "But it just might work."

I let go of the structure, and to everyone's surprise, it stayed upright.

Just.

Barely.

"Leave it like this," Melina whispered. "Don't even touch it."

I was so afraid it would fall I actually held my breath.

"Thirty seconds left," Coach Carter said. "And don't forget that you need to balance the marshmallow on top. No marshmallow means instant disqualification."

Shoot! We'd totally forgotten about the marshmallow.

In what felt like no time at all, he began the final countdown. "Ten seconds... nine seconds... eight seconds..."

Siarra handed me the marshmallow.

"Five seconds... four seconds... three seconds..."

"Just place it gently inside the spaghetti," Nicole said.

I didn't listen to her. Instead, I stabbed the marshmallow into the tallest strand of spaghetti.

Coach Carter blew his whistle. "Hands up!"

Time went into slow motion as I glanced around the room. All the students were raising their hands and stepping away from their structures.

I did likewise, releasing our marshmallow and stepping back—

Noooooo! I gasped in horror as our sad-looking spaghetti tower toppled over, sending our marshmallow bouncing onto the floor.

My team let out a collective sigh, and I leaned on my desk, feeling sick to my stomach. There was a strange buzzing inside my ears.

It was all over.

The spaghetti tower was a metaphor of my life— both had completely fallen apart right in front of my eyes.

"Sorry, Taylor," Coach Carter said. "Your team is out."

He moved quickly from one group to another, measuring each structure and calling out the height.

"And with a structure measuring eighteen inches, we have a winner!"

It made perfect sense for Jake Murphy's team to win. He and his friend Matt were probably the two smartest kids in the whole school.

This made me feel a little bit better, but not for long, because Coach Carter asked Jake to tell the class about his team's winning strategy.

"We tried a few different things," Jake said, "then settled on a triangular structure, like an Egyptian pyramid..."

At the word *pyramid*, something sank in the pit of my stomach.

Jake's team won using the same idea Nicole had suggested.

I asked to be excused and left the room.

12

INVISIBLE

I stood in front of the mirror in the girls' washroom and examined my reflection. I barely recognized myself. Puffy eyes, pale skin—I looked tired and worn out, defeated.

And it wasn't even lunchtime yet.

I splashed water on my face and dried it with a paper towel. Why was I making so many bad choices lately? Why couldn't I do anything right? What had changed?

Nicole is what changed.

She'd turned my whole life upside down. *She* was the problem.

But when I looked up, I realized that wasn't true. The ugly truth was right there staring back at me.

CLANG! The bathroom door flew open, and a bevy of girls rushed in and gathered around the sinks to adjust themselves in the mirror. Bags, purses, and pockets revealed every accessory imaginable. Hairbrushes. Clips. Braids. Makeup. Phones. One girl pulled out a lighting rig, as if she were about to make a Hollywood movie.

TikTok girls. That's what everyone called them, because every spare moment went into making short videos of themselves.

A lot of kids thought they were phonies. That they never showed their real selves, only projecting what they wanted people to see.

But didn't we all do that?

We all wanted to be seen. No one wanted to be invisible. Especially not me.

And didn't we all want people to see us the way we imagined ourselves? Maybe we were the phonies, and these girls were the honest ones.

Who knew? But one thing I knew for sure, I wasn't being honest with anyone, especially myself. None of my problems were Nicole's fault. She was just trying to make friends and fit in at a new school. She was being herself, and I was being a total jerk.

I looked at my reflection in the mirror again. I didn't look as bad as I'd thought. In fact, there was a new sparkle in my eyes and some color had come back into my cheeks.

Not wanting to waste any more time hiding out in the girls' bathroom, I pushed past the TikTok girls and through the heavy door, determined to find Melina and apologize.

She was waiting at our usual lunch spot outside, and instead of mad, she looked worried.

"Are you okay?" she asked.

"I'm much better now," I said. "I needed to take a minute to pull myself together."

"What's going on with you lately? You've been acting so different."

"I'm sorry," I said again, searching for the right words. "It's not you."

"But it's like you're mad at everybody, including me. And I have no idea what I did wrong."

"You didn't do anything wrong," I said. "Well, not really..."

"What does that mean?"

"Nothing." I wasn't ready to get into the whole Nicole stealing my best friend thing yet. "I'm still upset about basketball."

"Ugh, basketball," she muttered. "Of course."

We walked in silence for a minute, then stopped at

the edge of the school property and leaned against the wire fence.

I looked back toward the school. The yard was filled with kids of all ages, talking and laughing and fooling around. It was loud, but the noises were familiar and comforting.

"Remember that sleepover when I ate all the sour candies and got sick?" I asked.

She chuckled. "Yeah. You puked your guts out."

"I knew I was going to be sick, but I still kept eating."

Melina gave me a confused look.

I was confused too. I wasn't sure exactly why this story was important. But it was like a clue I needed to decipher.

"I knew it was wrong," I continued. "I knew it was a bad idea, but I did it anyway."

Melina raised an eyebrow. "It was just candy."

"I know," I said, shaking my head. "But it's like lately I keep eating more and more candy. I know I'm making bad decisions, but I can't stop myself."

As if on cue, I saw Nicole walking in the distance. She looked so lost and lonely, I felt sorry for her. And ashamed of myself.

"You're not really making any sense," Melina said. "If you know you shouldn't do something, don't do it."

I tried to lighten the mood by making a joke. "Duh, why didn't I think of that?"

Melina noticed Nicole and waved her over, and I felt a sudden urge to run away. I'd always preferred hanging out with friends one-on-one, and Melina and I had been a twosome for so long... Maybe I just wasn't ready for things to change.

I didn't want to say or do anything else stupid, but unfortunately, my brain had other ideas. As soon as Nicole reached us, I waved at her and blurted out, "I've got to pee!"

I strode past her, then practically sprinted back inside the school.

13

OUR FIRST GAME

Over the next two weeks, I tried to keep my jealousy in check during practices. It was hard, but I felt like I was making some good progress.

I was still fairly cold to Nicole, but I dutifully passed her the ball—when there was no other choice—and I tried not to lose my temper. I even kept my glares and dirty looks to a minimum. There were still a lot of eye rolls, but overall, things seemed to be getting better.

And then our first game of the season arrived.

To be honest, the team was doing great so far. Nicole had already scored twelve points. I had scored two. If we ran the plays the way Coach Carter had taught us, there was almost certainly no way we could lose.

And Nicole would score even *more* points.

I knew I should be happy that we were winning, but I wasn't. I was upset.

And since we were up by sixteen points, I decided to do something I'd never even considered before. Sabotage the game.

To be more specific, I decided to sabotage *Nicole's* game.

A point guard's main job was to set up the plays and put their teammates in the best possible position to succeed. Basically, I was supposed to get Nicole the ball and she was supposed to put it in the basket.

But instead, I did everything I could to ensure she *wouldn't* get the ball. Or, I gave her the ball when she couldn't possibly do anything with it.

Rule number seven on the official NBA website was all about the shot clock, a thirty-second countdown clock (twenty-four seconds for the pros in the NBA) that showed how much time the team possessing the ball had to get a shot off. It was meant to speed up the pace of the game. Players forgot about the shot clock all the time and were constantly losing possession over it.

So I watched the shot clock while dribbling the ball to keep it out of the other team's possession, and then I lobbed Nicole grenades. That was what they called it when a player passed the ball to a teammate with only five seconds left to shoot it.

This guaranteed Nicole wouldn't have enough time to move the ball and get off a quality shot.

Other times when I got the ball, instead of setting Nicole up with a good pass, I threw the ball at her feet, her shins—anywhere but where I was supposed to. And my passes were either too hard or too soft.

I did it a number of times, but Nicole never complained. In fact, she encouraged me and said, "Don't worry about it."

When the almost deafening sound of the final buzzer went off, we'd beaten the Mustangs by only eight points. It was a little close for comfort, but we'd won *and* I'd stopped Nicole from getting too many points.

We cheered the customary "Hip hip hooray!" three times for the other team, then ran over and formed a line to shake hands with our opponents. We said either "Good game" or "GG" as we passed each one, but most players rarely made eye contact.

Then we gathered back at the bench and congratulated ourselves on the win. After a few minutes of small talk, everyone gathered their things and headed out to meet their parents and go home.

"Taylor!" Coach Carter called.

I could tell by the look on his face that he wasn't happy with me. "I'm sorry, Coach," I said, walking up to him. "I didn't play my best. I know that."

"Stop it. You knew exactly what you were doing. You've never made a bad pass in your life."

He knew. Somehow, he knew.

"What do you mean?" I asked, feigning ignorance.

"You're *not* playing shooting guard. Do you understand?"

"Yeah, but—"

"Jealousy is like a virus," he said, cutting off my excuses. "If you let it take hold, it'll eat you up inside." He shook his head, barely able to look at me. "You have to live with the choices you make. And this type of behavior is completely unacceptable."

"Yeah, but—"

"No buts," he said firmly. "Forget about playing shooting guard. That's not happening."

"I'm sorry," I said. "I didn't mean to—"

"Wrong! You knew exactly what you were doing. That's why I'm so disappointed in you."

Coach's words hit me like a punch in the gut. And I must have looked really hurt, because his demeanor softened immediately.

"Basketball comes easy to you, Taylor. You have natural talent. That's a gift. But practicing your skills and learning new ones—that's hard work. It takes real effort. That's the choice you have to make. Do you coast? Or do you choose to work hard, learn new skills, and improve your game." He tilted his head and gave me a serious look. "Do you want to be a better basketball player?"

"Yes."

"Then you need to play for the name on the front of the jersey, not the one on the back. Do you understand what that means?"

I nodded.

"Good." He gave me a fist bump. "That's what I'm trying to help you do. You need to trust me, and you need to trust your teammates. You don't know everything. No one does. But great things happen when we work together. That's true in life and basketball."

We said our goodbyes and I trudged my way across the court toward the locker room, my head hung low.

Message received.

What was I thinking? I couldn't believe I had let things go so far. All because I was jealous of Nicole.

I would never sabotage another player again.

I would change my ways.

Unfortunately, changing my ways was going to be much harder than I thought.

14

OLD HABITS

Tuesday's practice was terrible, and today's session was turning into a complete disaster.

Coach had us playing a practice game, but nothing was going right. At least not for me. He'd given me explicit instructions not to shoot the ball. "Don't break the chain," he said. Every single time I touched the ball, I had to pass it to someone else. It made no sense. Everyone else on the team seemed to be improving, but I was playing worse than ever.

It was infuriating.

Not only was I a complete newbie in my position as point guard, without a clue how to play the position, it was like I had never seen a basketball in my life. Sad.

My team was getting destroyed by Nicole's team. It was a complete blowout. She had—*of course*—scored a billion points. Every time she touched the ball it went in the basket.

After fifteen minutes of fast play, Coach blew his whistle and yelled out, "Water break! Two minutes." Game play stopped and players hustled over to the bench for their water bottles.

"What's wrong, Taylor?" Coach asked, stepping in front of me as the other players walked off the court. "You look upset."

"No kidding," I replied. "You won't let me shoot the ball."

"You need to get better at setting up plays. Don't break the chain."

"But if I can't shoot, I can't score any points."

He smiled. "Exactly. You're supposed to help your teammates score points."

"There's no danger of *that* happening." Then under my breath, I added, "They all suck." I regretted the words the second they left my mouth, but it was too late.

"Watch yourself, Taylor!" Coach snapped. "Or you'll be warming the bench next game."

I tried to move past him, but he raised his hands, motioning for me to wait.

"You're team captain. Your teammates need to know they can trust you."

"So, I never get to win any games?" I asked.

"Individuals don't win games, teams do," Coach said, dropping his hands in exasperation.

Most of my team had finished grabbing water by now, and Siarra overheard Coach's last comment. "Teamwork is the dream work," she said, giving us a cheesy thumbs-up.

"Our team is a nightmare," I muttered, making sure no one else heard. Even I couldn't believe the words coming out of my mouth.

As the rest of my team walked up, Siarra, always the optimist, tried to lighten the mood. "We just haven't found our groove yet."

"We're definitely a little rough," Melina said. "But we'll get there."

Coach nodded. "Exactly. That's the spirit."

I couldn't believe it. I was captain, but my teammates were the ones giving the pep talk.

Nicole's team started toward our group, but Coach told them to go practice free throws for a minute and waved my team into a huddle.

"The problem," he said, motioning to the whole group. "Is that you're acting like single players instead of a whole team." Coach had given similar speeches many times during previous practices. It was no big deal.

But then he singled me out. "Taylor. You need to set the example."

It was unexpected, and I didn't appreciate it one bit. I was in no mood to be scolded, especially in front of the whole team.

"I do set the example," I said. "I'm the best player on my team, but you won't let me score any points."

"I, I, I," Coach said. "Listen to yourself, Taylor. This isn't all about you. You're part of a team. For you to get better, *they* have to get better."

When Coach got excited, he talked about basketball like it was a spiritual calling. I hoped this wasn't turning into another one of *those* talks.

I threw my hands up in the air. "Well, what am I supposed to do?"

"You need to pass the ball," he said. "Don't break the chain. Set up the plays we've been working on. Understand?"

"But if you just let me shoot, we could beat them."

Coach shook his head, then turned to the other players and quickly gave each one some pointers. Finally, he returned his attention to me. "Are you going to play your position or not?"

"Fine. I'll pass the ball more."

Coach looked at me with a serious expression. "If you take another shot, you'll be benched."

"What if I get possession?" I asked.

"You pass the ball."

"What if I'm in a good position?"

"Pass the ball," he repeated.

"But, what if I see the shot?" I pleaded, feeling desperate.

He motioned to the rest of the team and raised his hands like a conductor in front of an orchestra. And when he lowered his hands, the players spoke in unison, in time with each dramatic movement.

"PASS. THE. BALL," they said, then broke out laughing.

Coach called for the game to start up again, and all the players on my team were still laughing as we moved into our positions. Well, everyone except me.

It didn't make any sense, and it felt like I was being punished for no reason.

Was I a ball hog? Yes. Should I pass the ball more? Sure. Did I know the new plays? Um... not really.

Okay, maybe Coach did have a few reasons.

Still, did the punishment fit the crime? Would not letting me shoot really solve anything?

At the tip-off, Siarra knocked the ball back to me, and I dribbled past a couple of players and made my way into their key. I saw an opening, but Coach's "Don't break the chain" warning echoed in my head, so I faked a shot and passed the ball over to Melina. She fumbled my pass and Nicole stole possession.

"Come on!" I shouted, and raced back down the court. I was the only one hustling.

Nicole went on a fast break and scored with a bank shot.

I glared at her as she ran back, but she ignored me and wouldn't even make eye contact. This made me want to score on her team even more.

My team fell into a pattern. Once we had possession, I would work my way up the court and get inside the key. From there, I'd set up Siarra for the shot. I'd only pass to Melina as we moved up the court.

Apparently Coach Carter noticed, because after a few minutes of play, he blew his whistle and called me in for a time-out.

"Why aren't you letting Melina take any shots?" he asked.

"Because she throws a brick every time."

"Well, how do you expect her to get any better?"

"I don't know," I said, frustrated. It felt like I couldn't do anything right. "I can't control how other people play."

"Watch what she's doing. Try to help her get better. Encourage her. Let her take the shot. Otherwise, she'll never improve."

I pouted. "But she keeps missing."

"Don't worry if she misses. We've got to help her

build her confidence so she can make the shot during a real game."

I tried to do what Coach said, but the rest of the scrimmage was just as painful. Each play followed a similar pattern: I'd get the ball and pass it to a teammate. They'd usually mishandle it or miss the shot. Melina missed almost every shot I gave her. She seemed to be getting worse.

When Coach blew his whistle and ended the game, I let out a sigh of relief. *Finally.* My misery was over.

Everyone hustled over to the benches, and as Coach gave us his standard end-of-practice spiel, I glanced over at the faces of my teammates. Melina and Siarra were all smiles, as if we'd won today's game instead of lost. In fact, not one of my teammates seemed bothered by our loss at all.

What was the point if you didn't play to win? Was I the only one who cared? I could feel myself getting upset again.

Then Coach said a word that always caught my attention. *Ravens.* I felt my chest tighten and I took short, shallow breaths.

"Our first game against the Ravens is Saturday," he was saying. "They're a tough team, but if we follow our game plan—and don't break the chain—we'll do fine."

Nothing about Coach's plan made any sense to me. I

thought we were supposed to play to win, but how could we ever hope to beat the Ravens this way?

Let Melina take some shots? *Fine.* Let Nicole play shooting guard? *Fine.* But what about me? Why make me pass the ball every time? Why couldn't I score some points too?

And what if my family came to watch? Mom wouldn't care, but what would Dad think? And Jason?

I already knew the answer to that one.

He'd never let me live it down.

15

UNEXPECTED ENCOUNTERS

"You told me this was the last one," I heard Mom say.

"I know," Dad replied. "But it's really good money. We can finally get ahead of some of these bills."

Dad had got home last night, and he and Mom were having a talk in the kitchen. They were already mid conversation when I started listening from the hallway.

Jason and Baby Gemma were both still in bed.

"But you just got back. The kids miss you. I miss you."

"I know, sweetheart. I miss you guys too. This isn't easy for me either."

I heard Mom mixing something in a bowl. Probably pancakes—Dad loves them.

"I don't know how we can make it work," she said.

"I'm exhausted. I can't do it all on my own. And the kids need you here."

"We need to think about what this money could do for us."

"And what happens when you get offered another gig? And another one after that? You'll be gone all the time."

Dad sighed. "Maybe I can get back on weekends. I don't know. I haven't figured everything out yet."

There was a pause, then Dad said in a lighter tone, "Do you know what else I'm trying to figure out?"

Silence...

I leaned in closer. What was it? What else was he trying to figure out? Wasn't this all bad enough?

"AHA!" he yelled, leaping out and landing in the hallway right in front of me.

"Ahh!" I screamed.

"Which kid is snooping on us!" He grabbed me and lifted me up in the air. "Come here, you little stinker," he said, pulling me into a big, beautiful hug.

"Daddy!" It felt so good to see him. I'd missed him so much. The thought of him leaving again almost made me cry.

"Are you coming to my game today?" I blurted out. "We're playing the Ravens—the meanest team in the league." The words sounded a little childish coming out of my mouth, but I didn't care. This was important to me.

"I wouldn't miss it for the world," he said, then set me back down.

I squeezed him as hard as I could, pressing my face against his chest so he wouldn't see my tears.

Soon, Baby Gemma and Jason woke up, and we all feasted on pancakes with syrup and had a wonderful morning.

I hoped it was a sign that the rest of the day would go just as well.

When it was time to leave for the game against the Ravens, I was filled with conflicting emotions—nervous about playing point guard, but excited to have everyone watching and cheering me on from the stands.

Then at the last minute, Jason decided he didn't want to go.

Of course. He just had to go and make today about him.

"Come on, Jason," Dad said. "It'll be fun."

"It's our first family outing all together in a long time," added Mom.

"And our last," Jason muttered.

"Let's not get into that again right now," Dad said. "You're coming. We can talk more about things tonight." He placed his arm around Jason's shoulder, but Jason shrugged it off. He was taking Dad's leaving again pretty hard.

"Come on," Mom pleaded. "Do it for Taylor."

"I'll score some points just for you," I said.

Jason reluctantly agreed to join us and we were on our way. Finally.

Western Elementary, home of the Ravens, was tall and intimidating. It looked more like a castle than a school, with big gray bricks, long thin windows, and two massive oak doors at the entrance. A huge banner fluttered from the rooftop.

If I thought my stomach was filled with butterflies before, now it was overflowing.

After Dad parked the car, Jason pulled me aside as our parents walked ahead. "Don't let it intimidate you, Toes. You're the best. Don't forget it."

"Thanks, Jason," I said, nodding. I wasn't sure I believed it anymore, but it was nice to hear it from him. That was the weird thing about Jason—when he wasn't being a complete jerk, he was actually a great brother.

I was happy he'd decided to come, and I wanted to impress him and Dad, show them exactly what I could do. But as point guard, that wouldn't be easy.

I stopped walking and took his arm. "Jason," I whispered. "Coach wants me to pass the ball every time I get it."

"What? You're a great shooter. That makes no sense."

"I know, right? But now I'm supposed to set everyone else up to score."

"Forget *that*." Jason snorted. "What does he know? If you see a shot, take it! That's how you win games."

"I'm not sure..."

He looked me right in the eyes. "If you want to be the best, you've got to look out for yourself."

"But he's the coach."

"Do you want to win or not?" he asked, folding his arms over his chest.

"Yeah, I want to win."

"Then go for it. If you put enough points on the board, no one is going to care. Especially not Coach Carter."

We hustled up the rest of the walkway to catch up to Dad, who was holding the door for us.

"Getting some last-minute pointers?" he said.

I nodded and entered the school.

But once inside, I became even more nervous. Ravens posters and banners were everywhere. There was no escape.

A volunteer directed us to the large, state-of-the-art

gymnasium. It was awe-inspiring, with championship banners from previous years hanging from the rafters and bleachers on either side of the court that were already filling up with students, parents, and families.

Ravens fans had almost filled their section of the bleachers—there were hardly any seats left—and the Tiger's side looked almost empty by comparison, with only a few small groups sprinkled across the large open section.

Mom and Dad each gave me a hug, then went chasing after Baby Gemma, who had taken the opportunity to run off. Jason wished me luck and reminded me one last time to "take the shot."

There was still time before the game tip-off, so instead of joining Coach and the rest of the team, I made my way back outside to find a bathroom. I was nervous enough without worrying about having to pee in the middle of a game.

Once I'd finished, I stayed seated inside the stall, wanting to take a moment to calm my nerves and collect my thoughts.

Suddenly, I heard the bathroom door burst open and someone rush in. I stayed quiet and peered out through a crack in the door.

A girl wearing a Tigers uniform leaned over the sink and splashed water on her face. When she lifted her head to look in the mirror, I recognized the big, bushy hair immediately. Nicole.

Careful to remain hidden, I quietly leaned forward for a better look.

The door opened again and a girl wearing a Ravens uniform entered. She was followed by two more players who stayed back and watched the door, like bodyguards. At first, I thought they might be Nicole's friends, but she didn't look happy to see them at all.

"I thought I recognized that ratty hair," the girl said in super fake, overly friendly tone. The other girls remained silent.

"What do you want, Rachel?" Nicole said, looking like a caged animal desperate to escape. Her hand went to her necklace. I'd seen her play with it before and assumed it was her good luck charm, but maybe she touched it when she was nervous?

"Poor Nicole," Rachel said. "What's the matter? Are you not okay?"

Wow. Maybe Nicole's life wasn't so perfect after all.

I wasn't sure what was going to happen next, but I couldn't just sit there. I cleared my throat loudly and opened the stall door. "Hi, Nicole. Thanks for waiting for me."

I stepped between her and Rachel and quickly washed over my hands, then straightened up, trying to make myself as tall and imposing as possible. "Are these your friends?" I said as I grabbed a paper towel to dry my hands.

Rachel answered in her sickly-sweet voice. "Oh, yes. We were *very* close friends when Nicole went to school here."

"That's funny," I said, and took Nicole's hand. "She's never mentioned you."

"That *is* funny. Have you forgotten us already, Nicole? Well, I'm sure it'll all come back to you on the court."

One of the other girls opened the door for Rachel, and she strode out snickering, her friends following close behind.

Nicole looked embarrassed and muttered. "Thanks."

There was an awkward silence as we waited a minute to make sure the girls were really gone. Nicole took a deep breath. I opened the door and made sure the coast was clear before we left.

QUOTH THE RAVENS

So far, the Ravens were living up to their reputation as nasty players who were willing to do anything to win. They used every dirty trick in the book—pinching, poking, trash-talking, you name it.

And even though it was only the first quarter, they were already up by ten points.

Rachel was their lead scorer, a true force of nature. Like a tornado or a hurricane, she destroyed everything that got in her way—especially Nicole.

Rachel shut her down at every turn.

Wherever she went, Rachel followed, which completely threw Nicole off her game. She was totally flustered, making error after error, and hadn't scored a single point.

As the game progressed, instead of feeding the ball

to Nicole, I passed it to Siarra. She wasn't as good as Nicole, but she was the best I had. At least she had her head in the game. And despite missing as many shots as she took, she'd scored most of the points for our team.

I struggled to get Jason's words out of my head.

Take the shot, Taylor. Take the shot.

It was hard, but I ignored his advice and continued setting up plays and passing the ball. Never breaking the chain, exactly like Coach wanted. There were plenty of openings, but I didn't take them. Coach's instructions still echoed inside my mind.

Pass the ball. Pass the ball. Pass the ball.

But most of the time, my teammates fumbled the pass and lost possession.

Rachel jogged over to Nicole and said something—I couldn't hear what—but it had an immediate effect on Nicole. Her face sank and what little energy she had left drained out completely.

And Rachel wasn't the only player trash-talking Nicole. The entire Ravens team did it too, every chance they got. And it wasn't gentle ribbing or playful teasing. It was mean—like they were sworn enemies instead of old friends.

Maybe they were upset that she was playing for us? I could understand being sad or disappointed if a friend left and played for another team, but it seemed like more than that. Especially considering what happened in the bathroom.

Coach called a time-out, and we all huddled around him as he gave Nicole a pep talk. "... I know it's hard, Nicole, but you can do this."

Maybe *he* knew what was going on. It seemed like he knew *something*.

"They're trying to shut down Nicole," he said to the rest of us. "Let's help her out." He gave each player some quick feedback, but didn't offer me much. "Keep it up," he said. "Don't break the chain."

"Can I take some shots?"

"Not yet. I need you to keep passing the ball, especially to Nicole."

I shook my head. "I keep giving her the ball, but she's afraid to take the shot."

Coach gave me a disappointed look and turned to Nicole. "You can handle this," he said. "Don't let them take this game from you. We've all got your back." He glared back at me. "Right?"

The entire team nodded, and so did I.

When game play resumed, so did our problems. I followed Coach's instructions and passed Nicole the ball every chance I got. But as soon as she had it, she handed it off to someone else. The ball was like a hot potato to her and the whole team was suffering because of it.

I glanced up at the bleachers and saw Jason shaking his head. He caught my eye and raised his hands to shoulder height, as if to say "What's going on?"

I shrugged back.

"Take the shot!" he yelled out, but Mom and Dad shushed him immediately.

Was he right?

Mom, Dad, and Jason were watching us get our butts kicked, watching me just let it happen. Would they be disappointed in me?

What if I followed Coach's plays, but set up the shots for myself? Nicole wasn't going to take them—maybe it was time for someone else to step up?

I dribbled up the court, wondering how I was supposed to help the team if I couldn't score any points. I pivoted around my defender, saw an opening, and moved toward the basket. But at the last minute, instead of taking the shot, I passed the ball back to Melina.

Melina lined up her shot and released the ball, but I could tell it would miss before it even bounced off the rim. Another brick. It wasn't the first, and it probably wouldn't be the last.

I sprinted over and scooped up the rebound, then scanned the area for someone to pass the ball to. But there was no one. Siarra was out of position, and Nicole wasn't even paying attention.

Enough!

I couldn't let this continue.

So I settled in and took the shot. *Swish*. Two points.

That one basket was all it took—I was hooked. The original Taylor was back and up to her old tricks. If I got the ball, I kept it. Instead of passing, I showboated my way through their defense.

The Ravens didn't know what hit them. I darted in and out of players like they were standing still. Rachel was still covering Nicole, which left me wide open to score again and again.

Coach gave me a few dirty looks, but I didn't care. We were back in the game. And if I continued like this, I might be able to close their lead and catch up before the half.

The Ravens made a run for the basket, and I exploded toward the ball like a cannon. I was everywhere, shutting them down at every turn. They tried to make a long pass, but the receiver flubbed the ball and it rolled away.

Completely focused on getting possession, I sprinted for the ball like my life depended on it. Another player reached the ball at almost exactly the same time, but I grabbed it with both hands, planted my right foot, and spun around.

The crowd gasped, then went quiet.

The ball was mine! I sprinted down the court—no one could catch me. Alone under the hoop, I jumped up and made the layup.

My old sneakers made a loud squeak when I landed. Then, I heard something else.

Crying?

I turned around and saw everyone huddled around Nicole. She was sitting cross-legged at center court—her head tilted backward, a bloody towel under her nose.

Oh no! Did I steal the ball from my own teammate?

My elbow must have come up and smashed into her nose when I yanked the ball away. But I didn't do it on purpose. I wanted to win, but I never meant to hurt her.

I ran over to apologize, but I couldn't get very close. "I'm so sorry, Nicole!" I called out. "It was an accident!"

Melina gave me a disappointed look, and Siarra made a weird face at me. Did they think I'd hurt Nicole on purpose?

Players hovered nearby as Coach Carter, the school nurse, and a concerned parent helped Nicole to her feet. It might have been her mother, but I wasn't sure.

I shuffled my way in closer and tried to explain myself again. "It was an accident! I didn't do it on purpose."

"Taylor, enough," Coach said, raising a hand. "Please

go take a seat on the bench. We need to make sure Nicole is okay."

They couldn't think I did it on purpose, could they? That's not who I am. Everyone knows that. Don't they?

I was about to say something else, but caught myself. Coach was right. Nicole was hurt, and I shouldn't be making this about me. I wasn't the victim.

But what if I was the villain? That's probably what it looked like to everyone else.

I watched the nurse help Nicole off the court and out of the gym, wishing for her to be okay.

Please don't have a broken nose! Please!

I slunk over to our bench with my head hung low. I couldn't bear to look up at my parents in the bleachers. It felt like the whole crowd was staring at me—and not in a good way. What was that old saying? *If looks could kill...*

Wishing I were invisible, I glanced across at the rest of my team. They looked scared. Were they afraid of me?

"It was an accident!" I said when Coach returned.

"We know." He paused and shook his head. "But I need you to take off that wristband."

"But—" I started, then sighed and took it off. Coach took the wristband from me and put it in his pants pocket.

When the ref blew the whistle for play to resume, I

glanced up and caught Rachel looking at me. Smirking, she golf clapped, quietly tapped the fingers of one hand against the palm of the other. I put my head in my hands and sat in silence for the rest of the game.

It was an accident. I am not a villain. I'm not a monster.

I needed to show everyone who I really was. And if they gave me another chance, that was exactly what I was going to do.

17

A SECOND CHANCE

The rest of the weekend went by in a blur. Everyone had an opinion on what happened, and I had long, hard conversations with everyone from Coach and my parents to Melina and Siarra. Every time I apologized, memories of the event flooded back. I hoped more than anything that Nicole would be all right.

I had apologized so many times, to so many people, that I was worried I might start sounding insincere. But I definitely wasn't. I was really, really sorry. And I was determined to make it up to everyone on the team. Especially Nicole.

If I ever got the chance.

She hadn't come back to the game on Saturday, and she didn't show up for school on Monday—which fueled even more speculation. Was her nose broken?

Was she completely disfigured? Was she ever coming back?

I'd wanted everyone to see me as a hero, but instead I was the villain. It had happened so fast. And it didn't seem fair.

Was I a hero? Definitely not. Was I a villain? Not entirely. At least I didn't think so. Selfish? Yes. Absolutely. One hundred percent. Could I change? Well, that remained to be seen—but I was determined to find out.

I had my work cut out for me, though. At home. At school. And definitely on the basketball court.

Tuesday morning I got up early, made my own breakfast, and took Poppy for a walk before practice.

I was first to arrive, even earlier than Coach Carter. And when he got there, I begged him to let me stay on the team and make it up to everyone. He agreed to give me another chance, but said I was benched until further notice, even during practices.

"I know I have a lot of work to do," I said. "I'll do whatever it takes."

He handed me a large, wide broom and had me start by sweeping the entire gymnasium. Next I lugged out all the basketballs, which were stored on a big rack with wheels, and set up the small orange cones. When players began arriving, Coach told me to start handing out the basketballs.

Most of my teammates took their ball in silence. Even Melina only grunted a hello.

Everyone was obviously still upset, and rightfully so. But at least Siarra smiled at me when she took her ball. That gave me a little hope.

I glanced at the gym's main entrance, hoping to see Nicole walk in. But no such luck. Had she quit the team? No, Melina would have told me.

Nicole was definitely the best player on our team—I could admit that now. She had speed, moves, and skill. If anything, her weakness was literally the opposite of mine. She passed the ball *too* much, and she didn't always take the shot, even when she should.

Coach ran a typical practice, and as I watched my teammates go through the usual drills, I decided that instead of focusing only on their weaknesses, I'd look for their strengths as well.

Melina's strength was her tenacity. She never gave up, and she'd stay on her player no matter what. If the person she was defending got away from her, she'd work hard to catch up to them again. Her main weakness was that she still telegraphed all her moves. That and she couldn't make a layup.

Emma's strength was her speed. She was like a rocket. I hadn't noticed it before, but then, I hadn't noticed a lot of things before. Her weakness was her lack of confidence. When she made a mistake, she got really upset with herself, which caused her to make even more mistakes.

Siarra was tall and fit and seemed to have boundless energy. She was a good all-around player. She could run, pass, and shoot. If she had a weakness, it was a lack of intensity. She didn't have that competitive instinct—it was all fun to her.

But the more I thought about it, the less I saw this as a weakness. Maybe all of us, especially me, could learn something from her. Then again, she was *so* nice she didn't like to see anyone lose. I'd never even seen her steal the ball away from another player. *That* was a weakness for sure.

Zoe's strength was passing. She was like a sharp-shooter when she passed the ball. Unfortunately, she was slow and didn't have much hustle.

Pari's strength was her grit. She never gave up. Unfortunately, she didn't understand the nuances of the game and fouled players constantly. If she were a starter, she wouldn't last one half without fouling out.

Lola's strength was her rebounding—she was always

in the right place at the right time—and her weakness was her lack of speed.

Sophie and Sarah were twin sisters and had no strengths on the court. They didn't even want to be there. Their parents made them play and it showed. There wasn't much I could do about that.

I approached Melina and offered to help her with her layup. "You've almost got it," I said.

She glared at me. "Yeah, right."

"No, really," I added. "You've got the footwork right —you're just jumping too soon." I walked under the hoop and placed a cone where I thought she should jump. "Take a run, but wait until you pass the cone to jump."

She shrugged. "It couldn't hurt." She stepped back and took a short run at the basket, waiting until she passed the cone before jumping. She was too close when she released the ball and it clanged against the rim.

"Yes!" I caught the rebound and tossed it back to her. "Now, release the ball a little bit sooner."

She repeated the process and missed again. But we adjusted each time, and she got closer and closer with each attempt. Finally, on the sixth try, it went in.

"Nice!" I yelled, clapping my hands while Melina beamed with pride and excitement. I hadn't seen her smile that big since her parents took us on our first pony ride. "Now let's see if you can get two in row."

And on the very next try, she did.

Melina wasn't the only one having fun. Her excitement was contagious, and I couldn't remember the last time I'd enjoyed a practice so much. She missed more than a few layups, but that didn't matter. She was on her way.

When Coach blew his whistle, I couldn't believe how fast the time had gone. I'd started the day dreading practice, and it had turned out to be one of the best ever. Melina and I were practically giddy as we made our way back to the bench.

After Coach gave a few quick notes, the other players headed off to class. I stayed behind to help put everything away, first collecting all the cones and putting the balls back onto the rack, then pushing and lugging everything over to the storage area beneath the stage.

"Thanks," Coach said.

"Thank you for giving me another chance."

"You're welcome." He began to close up the storage room. "It was nice to see you helping another player out."

"Yeah." I grinned. "It felt really good."

I dashed out of the gym and took the stairs up to our classroom two at a time. I had faced my problems head on and made some really positive choices. It felt like I was heading in the right direction.

I was determined to show Coach that I'd learned my lesson. "I'll show him how valuable I can be," I said out loud to the empty stairwell. I had a new goal now. I'd do everything I could to help the team make the tournament.

There was still time. I'd been given a second chance to turn my life around and I wasn't going to waste it. I felt happy and hopeful...

And then I entered the classroom.

18

OUCH!

Nicole was back.

Or at least what was left of her.

Her face was swollen, and she had dark, black bruises under her eyes and a large bandage taped across her nose.

Ouch.

There was a group of kids standing around her talking. When they noticed me, the whole room went silent.

Double ouch!

It was the first time we'd seen each other since the game. Since the moment I'd ruined everything.

I was overwhelmed with emotions. Shame. Sadness. Embarrassment. Anxiety.

I could only imagine what Nicole must have been feeling. Humiliation? Anger? Bitterness?

I panicked and ran out of the classroom, passing Coach Carter as I sprinted down the hallway to the nearest bathroom.

Once inside, I stared at my reflection in the mirror.

I think I get it now, what Nicole must have been feeling before the game against the Ravens.

There was a knock, and Coach Carter called through the door. "Taylor? Are you okay? Come out and talk to me."

I slowly opened the door and stepped into the hall. "I'm okay. But seeing her face..." I hung my head. "It looks so bad. I can't believe I did that. I feel terrible."

"Let's not rehash all that. It was an accident. It's going to be okay."

"Everyone thinks I'm a monster."

"You made a mistake. A lot of mistakes. It's going to take some hard work to repair the damage."

"You can say that again," I muttered.

"Did you think it was going to be easy?" he asked sharply.

"No, but—"

"Again with the 'no, buts,'" he said, cutting me off. He shook his head, but gave me a patient smile.

"I'm trying—"

"Good. Keep it up."

"What else can I do?" I asked as we arrived at the classroom door.

He opened it and motioned for me to enter, then said, "Take it one step at a time."

As I walked into the classroom, I could feel everyone's eyes on me, but I kept my head down and hurried to my seat. "I'm so sorry," I whispered to Nicole as I slid into my chair. "It was an accident."

She sat rigid, looking straight ahead. Complete silence. *Triple ouch!*

Keeping my eyes forward, I notice that Coach Carter had written the phrase "symbiotic relationships" across the white board in big black letters.

"There are four main symbiotic relationships," he began, and added four more words, saying each one as he wrote it. "Mutualism... commensalism... parasitism... and competition."

He gave us a short lecture that explained each symbiotic relationship within different ecosystems, then announced, "We're going to get into groups and write up some examples of each." He assigned everyone to a group—putting me with Melina, Siarra, and Nicole— and gave each group a large poster board and five colored pens. Memories of the Marshmallow Challenge fiasco flooded my mind.

Déjà vu–ouch!

Melina and Siarra were the first to push their desks together. Melina noticed Nicole's rigid posture and tried to cheer her up. "Come on. It's better than math." Then, remembering Nicole actually liked math, added, "Well, at least for us."

"Yeah," said Siarra, placing the board and pens on Nicole's desk. She put the black pen under her nose like a mustache and made a duck face. "It'll be lotsa fun."

Melina wrinkled her nose. "I'm not sure I get the assignment."

"We can divide the poster into four sections using the black pen," Siarra suggested, "and use a different colored pen for the examples."

"And the prettiest one wins," I added, stepping aside so Nicole could see. I wanted to show her that I was being inclusive, but maybe suggesting we make it a competition wasn't the best idea, considering.

Nicole hesitated, then said, "We could add little pictures next to each example."

"Yeah!" I said enthusiastically. "That's a great idea." And I meant it—it *was* a great idea.

"Okay..." Melina glanced around the group. "Do we each take a category, or work together?"

"There's no big rush," Nicole said. "So let's work together." She smiled shyly.

I caught her eye and smiled back at her. "What color do you want to start with?"

Before long, all four of us were laughing and joking around. Everybody was participating and helping each other out. We were allowed to use the class tablets to look up the examples, and I laughed out loud when I read the definition of "mutualism."

"What's so funny?" Melina asked.

"We're the perfect example of mutualism," I said. "Different types of people, but in a group where everyone benefits from the association."

"Um..." Siarra gave me a knowing wink. "You find the strangest things funny."

Melina and Nicole smiled at each other.

"Want to know what else I find funny?" I said.

Nicole nodded, and Melina said, "What?"

I held up a piece of paper with my drawing on it. "This is supposed to be a clown fish and an anemone."

All three of them looked at the drawing and burst out laughing. I hadn't drawn it badly on purpose, but there was no denying that it was terrible. It was probably the worst drawing of a clown fish and an anemone in the entire world.

"I *love* it," said Melina, giggling hysterically. "The perspective is so modern, so fresh."

Nicole laughed but didn't add anything else. She was

still nervous, and rightly so. I understood her reluctance to joke.

Siarra stroked her chin and squinted at the drawing. "The way you use colors. It's so... so..." She paused for dramatic effect. "So *terrible*! It's absolutely atrocious!"

"I know!" I snorted. "It looks like an orange cow trapped in a bowl of noodles."

"I think it's adorable," Nicole said.

"And they're not noodles," added Melina, pointing to the picture. "They're giant worms!"

We all laughed even harder.

"Settle down over there," Coach Carter said.

But it was obvious that he was just teasing. I could tell he was happy we were all getting along.

And so was I.

19

TRAINING

I arrived early again on Thursday to help Coach with whatever he needed. I tried to stay positive, but I was really worried about Nicole. *What if she doesn't come back to practice? What if she can't play anymore? What if I've ruined basketball for her forever?*

Coach Carter must have seen that I was worried, because he pulled me aside and let me know Nicole would be back at practice again soon. She was just taking some time off to heal.

I was so relieved by the news, I leaped up and hugged him. It felt like a huge weight had been taken off my chest and I could breathe again. I knew I still had a lot of work to do. But this was huge.

"It's going to be okay," he said.

And for the first time since the accident, I believed it.

I prepared for practice with a new sense of purpose. I was going to make things right. I was going to stop putting myself first all the time and actually try to be a leader. I was going to be the type of player and friend people could count on. And the first place I was going to start was helping Melina with her layups.

"You've really dialed it in," I said, catching the ball as it fell through the basket.

"Thanks for showing me."

"Can I show you something else?"

She nodded, so I continued. "Remember when you asked me how I always seemed to know what you were going to do?"

"Yeah."

"And I told you it's because you always telegraph your moves?"

"Show me," she said.

We were running through some of her most common mistakes, when someone cried out in pain.

Emma had misjudged a pass and jammed her fingers.

It happened to every basketball player at one point or another, and it usually wasn't too serious. But Coach's first aid kit wasn't cutting it. Emma was in tears and asking to be taken to the nurse's office.

"I'll be back in a few minutes," Coach said. "Taylor. Run some drills."

Thrilled that Coach was giving me this opportunity, I ran over and grabbed his whistle and clipboard off the bench.

The whistle was a shiny metal, and heavier than it looked. As I held it in my hand, a strange sensation washed over me. I felt special. Important.

I blew into it, and the players all rushed over.

"Is that Coach's whistle?" Melina asked.

"Ewww," said Siarra. "Gross. Taylor's using Coach's whistle!" Everyone laughed and started making gagging faces.

I laughed too. "Yeah, I guess it is pretty gross. But it's too late to stop now." I blew the whistle again. "Let's do some layup progressions."

And to my surprise, everyone listened to me.

I divided the players into three groups based on ability, each at their own basket. Dad had taught me and Jason this way, and it really worked. So I figured it might work for my teammates as well.

The first group of players didn't know the first thing about layups, so I lined them up and had each player start close to the basket and get low, ready to explode.

They'd take a step with their left foot, jump and shoot the layup, then pass the ball to the next player and go to the back of the line. Once they'd all had a shot, they moved to the opposite side and tried from there.

The second group of players were a little bit better, so I added a little more complexity.

During the Ravens game, I'd noticed our players had a bad habit on layups. They always swept the ball from the outside of their body to the inside. This made it much easier for the defender to steal the ball.

To fix this, I lined up the players on the right-hand side of the key. Then, as they stepped toward the basket, I had them start with the ball on their right hip and focus on keeping it on that side as they took the shot. This would help them shield the ball. Once they all had a shot, they moved to the left side and tried from there.

The third group of players consistently made their layups, so I had them work on their dribble layups. Instead of simply taking a step and shooting, they would dribble and take a few steps. The stronger the player, the further back they could start.

The groups practiced their assigned layups for about ten minutes, and I saw immediate improvements in some of them, especially Siarra and Melina. They were both getting better quickly and showing more confidence.

Melina was in the second group and was consistently making her shots. When she drained another one, I called out to her. "Melina! Move over to the next group." She grinned and ran over to join the others at the third basket.

Suddenly, I heard Coach Carter's voice behind me. "Now that's what I like to see! Looking good! Very good indeed."

"I was just keeping them warmed up for you, Coach." I held out his whistle and clipboard.

"No way," he said, refusing to take them. "You're doing great. Show us what other tricks you have up your sleeve."

It wasn't a huge gesture, but it meant the world to me. Coach trusted me and really believed I could help the team. I was so proud, I thought my chest would explode.

I blew the whistle and the players ran in.

I suggested a fast-break drill, another game I used to practice with Dad and Jason, then divided the players into two teams. Red and blue.

The game started as a three-on-two, then became three-on-three. Three red players started with the ball near midcourt, while two blue defensive players were stationed underneath the hoop. The remaining players stayed with their respective teams on the sidelines.

In the first round, Siarra and Melina were on opposing teams and were keen for some friendly competition.

"Bring it on," Siarra said. "Blue rules. Your team is going down!"

"In your dreams," Melina replied. "Red team all the way!"

On the whistle, Melina and her two red teammates started a fast break and tried to score. After thirty seconds, I blew the whistle and another blue player joined Siarra's team on defense. Once the red team scored, they switched over to defense and the blue team went on the attack. After each team had scored and defended once, new players were called in.

It was a fast-moving game and really fun to watch— even the players on the sidelines were engaged. There was laughing and cheering and even applause when someone made a nice shot.

I glanced over at Coach Carter and caught him smiling at me. He tapped his wristwatch, indicating that it was time for me to wrap things up, so I blew the whistle. I heard groans of disappointment that the game, and the practice, was over.

When everyone else ran off to get ready for class, I stayed behind and helped Coach put things away.

"How did that feel?" he asked.

"Amazing." I grinned. "I hardly missed playing at all."

"Well, don't get used to it."

"What do you mean? Did I do something wrong?"

"No, no," he said reassuringly. "Nothing like that. It's just that now you've got to figure out how to do the same thing while playing."

I let out a sigh of relief.

That was something I could handle. That was something I could figure out.

And I planned to do just that.

20

FAMILY SURPRISES

"You just don't get it," I heard Jason say from the living room.

I was standing with my back against the kitchen wall, listening in on yet another heated conversation.

"I get it," Mom replied. "I get that you think the whole world is against you. I get that you're angry Dad is away."

"I *am* angry Dad is away! He's *always* away, and it sucks!"

Mom's sigh was loud enough for me to hear. "Yes. It sucks for all of us."

"So why won't you cut me some slack?"

"I have!" she said sharply. "But enough is enough."

"What's that supposed to mean?" Jason snapped.

"I'm tired of you playing the victim all the time."

"I don't!"

"You do!"

"What do you want from me?" Jason yelled.

After a pause, Mom said softly, "I want you to start thinking about how to get things back on track."

"I am!" I heard him stomp out of the living room and slam the front door. The sound startled me and I bumped a chair, giving away my location.

Mom walked into the kitchen and shook her head at me. "You need to stop eavesdropping, Taylor."

"I'm sorry."

Baby Gemma started crying. The noise must have woken her up.

"Go see if *you* can talk to him," Mom said. "I need to get your sister."

"What can *I* do?" I asked, a bit shocked at the suggestion.

"I don't know. He's your brother and he's having a hard time. Try talking to him." She threw up her hands in exasperation, then hurried off to get Baby Gemma.

I didn't really know what to do either, so I did what I always did when I was stressed and confused. I grabbed the basketball and ran outside.

I caught up with Jason quickly, but since he still looked pretty upset, I stayed far enough back for him not to notice me.

I followed him for an entire block, but on the second block, I forgot I was trying to be quiet and dribbled the basketball once. I quickly caught it and tried to hide behind a tree, but he saw me.

"Come on out, Taylor. Let's go shoot some hoops."

I joined him, and we started walking to the school courts.

"You'd make a lousy spy," he said, snatching the ball from me. He was still in a bad mood, but he seemed better. A few games might help take his mind off things.

There was no one else on the court, so we played some one-on-one. I made him work for every point.

"Do you remember that time you beat me?" he asked, tossing me the ball and walking back to the line.

"Yeah. It was one of the best days of my life." I checked the ball.

"No one could get the last basket."

"I know," I said, waiting for him to make his move. But he just stood there, so I kept talking. "We'd been playing for hours, but you wouldn't let us quit until one of us won by two. It went back and forth for a long time. But then I dug deep and pulled off a crossover that put you on skates. It worked perfectly and set me up for an alley-oop layup off the backboard."

"I remember," he said, smiling. He dribbled the ball

a couple of times, but still didn't make a move for the net.

"It was the first time that move ever worked on you."

"First and last time." He gave me a long, strange look —squinting one eye and pursing his lips.

"What?" I demanded.

"Come on, Toes... think about it."

In a flash, my mind replayed parts of the game. The memories weren't exact, but I slowly pieced things together. "You let me win?"

"Yeah, but I made you work for it."

My throat tightened and my hands clenched into tight fists at my side. One of my most cherished memories was a lie.

"You *lied* to me?" The words came out angry and sad at the same time.

"I encouraged you," he corrected.

"You let me think I could beat you, but it was all just a big fat lie?"

"Yes," he said, "But after that day, you took your game to a whole other level."

"Why are you telling me this now, right before a game?" I asked.

"Do you know who Roger Bannister is?"

I shook my head.

"In the olden days, the four-minute mile was considered impossible, beyond human reach."

"Okay?" I had no idea what he was talking about.

"Well," he continued, "in 1954, Roger Bannister ran the mile in under four minutes. And soon people all over the world started beating the record too."

"Okay?" I said again, still confused.

"You needed to *believe* you could beat me. Once you smashed through that glass ceiling, the spell was broken and you started to give me a run for my money."

"So what are you saying?" I asked. "That I need to help my teammates *believe* they can win?"

He shrugged. "Maybe?"

"But I've been trying to encourage them. I want them to want it as much as I do. But they don't understand."

"Maybe you're the one who doesn't understand."

"What are you talking about? Nobody on that team understands basketball like I do."

"I watched you play against the Ravens," he said. "It reminded me of how intense I used to play."

"So what?"

"It's not always a good thing."

"You were a great player."

"But I wasn't a great *team* player," he said. "I never have been."

"What does this have to do with me?" I asked.

He shook his head. "Never mind. I think I'm just trying to convince myself."

"Convince yourself of what?"

"I don't know." His shoulders slumped. "That maybe I can change? That maybe it's not too late for me for turn things around?"

I'd been so wrapped up in my own problems, I hadn't realized how badly my brother was hurting. I wasn't an overly emotional person, but feelings of sadness and love overwhelmed me and I threw my arms around him. "Oh, Jason. It's not too late. It's not."

"It's okay." He gave me a little squeeze. "It's all going to be okay."

"Promise?" I said, wiping tears from my eyes.

"I promise." His eyes looked as red and puffy as mine probably did.

Jason grabbed the basketball off the ground and took one last shot. The ball arched perfectly in the air and went right in.

"Let's go home," he said. "It's almost time for your game. Who're you playing, anyway?"

"The Sharks. Are you coming?"

"If you want me to."

"Yes, of course I want you there!" I gave him another big hug.

As we walked home, I felt much better about my family. Maybe things would be okay.

Mom was in the living room when we got home. "Taylor," she said. "Jason and I need to talk. I want you go upstairs and clean your room. Start by making your bed."

"Now? The game starts in twenty minutes. We're going to be late."

"We're not leaving this house until it's done," she said, then gave me an odd grin.

I stomped up the stairs, so mad I wanted to scream, then threw open my bedroom door.

I gasped.

The room was spotless. Books and clothes were all put away, the desk was free of clutter and loose papers, and there was no garbage on the floor. Even the bed had been perfectly ma—

My eyes widened and the rest of my body froze when I saw what was on the middle of the bed.

An orange shoebox with a very famous white logo.

I stepped toward the box, heart racing, and slowly lifted the lid. And when I saw what inside, I screamed and burst into tears of joy.

A brand-new pair of sneakers! In the exact size and style that I'd been begging for.

21

RISE AND FALL

After the game against the Sharks—which we won—Nicole rejoined the team, wearing a fancy new face shield to protect her nose. Fortunately, the two of us were getting along much better, in class and on the court.

Practices were going well, and we were winning games and making our way up the standings. I was learning how to be a team player and follow Coach's plays. And after putting in some hard work, it felt like everyone on the team had finally forgiven me.

As team captain and point guard, I'd been pushing the team hard. Maybe I pushed some players a little *too* hard, but it was hard for me to tell sometimes what was going too far.

Case in point, if we maintained our lead in our

current game against the Bulls we'd make the tournament—I longed for a rematch against the Ravens—but since Nicole was still playing cautiously, I had to focus most of my attention on Siarra.

So when she lost possession and the Bulls scored, I called for a time-out and reprimanded her. "Why weren't you covering your player?"

"She's too fast," she said, breathing hard. "My ankle is bugging me. I can't keep up with her."

"We need you out there, Siarra."

She rotated her ankle and winced. "I think I should sub out."

"There's only a couple minutes left," I said, placing an encouraging hand on her shoulder. "We can hold them back."

Melina narrowed her eyes at me. "She's been playing hard. Give her a break, Taylor."

The ref motioned that our time-out was almost over.

I looked at Siarra intently. "If you dig down, I know you can do this. The team really needs you."

She sighed. "Okay."

Once play resumed, I immediately regretted pushing Siarra into playing. I could tell she wasn't her normal self, but before I got a chance to intervene, there was a scuffle under the basket and she went down. Hard.

Coach came running over. "Are you okay?" he asked, then helped Siarra over to the bench.

"Taylor pushed her to play with a sore ankle," Melina called out, shooting me a nasty look.

Coach subbed in two players, one for me and one for Siarra, and motioned to the ref for play to continue. "Taylor," he said. "Grab some instant ice packs from the first aid kit."

Argh! I need to be on the court!

I ran over and grudgingly did as he said, then sat down on the bench next to Siarra, who was massaging her sore ankle.

I handed her an ice pack. "Sorry. I didn't think it was that bad."

"No," Coach corrected. "You were only thinking about winning."

"It's okay," Siarra said. "I should've listened to my gut and subbed out. You were just trying to help us win."

The Bulls scored another basket and narrowed our lead to only four points. And even with an injured friend sitting next to me, all I could think about was winning. I should've been more empathetic, but instead I asked Coach to put me back in.

"You're not playing, Taylor."

"But we'll lose!"

"You've *already* lost," Coach snapped.

His comment didn't even register. "Well, if we beat the next team, we can still make the playoffs."

Coach shook his head and sighed. "How can you still not get it? Maybe you need to sit out the next game too."

I was so confused. "You're mad at me because I still want to win?"

"No," he said. "I'm frustrated because you still want to win *at any cost*. You put winning ahead of your teammate. That may be how the Ravens play, but that's not how *we* play."

With me and Siarra on the bench and Nicole not playing her best, the Bulls were able to rally. I watched in anguish as they scored two more baskets to tie, then won the game in the last minute of play.

One more loss, and we wouldn't make the tournament.

22

COULD THINGS GET ANY WORSE?

The next afternoon, I finished all my homework and walked Poppy. But I still felt anxious, so I grabbed my basketball and trudged my way across the field to the school courts.

I took a few shots. Nothing went in. It was like the ball was cursed.

I tried to remember the feelings of joy I used to get playing basketball, but all I felt was stressed. I'd messed things up *again*. Was it even worth it to try?

I thought I was heading in the right direction, but things were worse now than they'd ever been. I wasn't shooting guard. I had no chance to win MVP. Coach was totally disappointed. And all my friends were angry with me. Again.

Maybe I should just quit?

I decided to practice my trick dribble, but the ball hit my foot and bounced away. I sighed, then looked up and saw Jason walking over to pick up the basketball.

"Hey, Toes," he said, dribbling the ball a few times before tossing it back to me. "It can't be *that* bad."

"Coach says I might have to sit out the next game. My teammates and my best friend are all mad at me." I took a shot. It wasn't even close.

He caught the rebound and made a face. "Okay, maybe it is that bad."

"I've ruined everything."

"We're a fine pair, eh?" he said. "What happened?"

"That's just it," I replied truthfully. "All I did was push the team to win."

He dribbled and took a shot that bounced off the backboard and went right in, then quickly moved to the basket and caught the ball before it even hit the ground.

"Maybe you were pushing too hard?" he suggested, tossing me the ball. "It's supposed to be fun."

"*Winning* is fun." I took my shot, but it hit the rim and made a distinct *THUNK* sound. I chased after it and threw it back to Jason. "Why am I the bad guy for wanting to win?"

"Maybe wanting to win isn't the problem," he replied, and sunk another shot. He was really good.

"You're the one who's always talking about digging deeper. Always taking the shot. Never giving up."

"That's true." He tilted his head at me. "But do you really want to follow my example?"

"I don't know what I want anymore," I said. "I just wish things could go back to the way they used to be."

Jason sighed. "Me too, kid. Me too."

It started to rain.

"Perfect timing," he said, going to grab the ball. "Come on." He looked back and motioned for me to walk with him. "Mom and Dad want to have a talk with us."

"Dad's home?" That was a surprise.

"Yeah," he replied, sounding worried. "Mom sent me a text."

I joined him and we walked toward home. "What do they want to talk about?" I asked.

"I don't know. But I doubt it's anything good."

"Do you think Mom and Dad are getting a divorce?"

"I don't know. Maybe? Money's been really tight lately."

"Are we gonna lose the house?"

"I don't know!" he barked.

It was raining harder now, but we walked slowly. Neither of us were in a hurry to receive any more bad news.

I stopped and lifted my head toward the sky, letting the rain splash across my face. I didn't want Jason to know I was crying. But he came over, wrapped his arms around me, and gave me the biggest, sweetest, longest hug ever. I felt safe. Loved.

I cried the rest of the walk home. And Jason wiped something from his own eyes more than once.

"Let's get this over with," he said, opening the front door.

I took his hand in mine. "I'm scared."

He gave my hand a gentle squeeze, and we entered the house.

23

NICOLE'S STORY

At lunchtime on Monday, I sat alone against the school fence where Melina and I usually hung out. She was away on a trip with her grandparents and would be missing the whole week of school, not to mention two important practices.

Melina was my best friend, and I missed her even though I knew she was still mad at me, but I was fine being alone. Besides, this would give me time to figure out how to convince Coach to let me play on Saturday. I wanted to play so we could make it to the tournament, but mostly because Mom and Dad said they'd both come.

I'd been so worried about my parents getting a divorce, or us maybe losing the house because of money troubles, but when they sat me and Jason down to talk yesterday, they'd been in really great moods. They apologized for the recent fighting and all the stress they'd caused. Then, they gave us the good news.

Dad had been offered a permanent job teaching music at the local college, and had accepted. He would still get to do what he loved—play music—but now he'd be able to do it close to home. And for the most part, our money troubles would be over. The whole family was ecstatic. Even Jason seemed happy.

I looked across the field and noticed Nicole walking. She was alone too. I'd done my best to repair our relationship after her accident, but she was really cold to me this morning in class. Not that I blamed her. I just kept messing up. It must've been hard to start over at a new school, and I certainly hadn't made things very easy for her. But maybe I could start now?

I got up and walked toward her. "How's it going, Nicole? You coming to practice tomorrow?"

"Yeah. I'll be there."

I joined her and did my best to keep the conversation going as we walked. "If we want to make the tournament, we need to be ready for Saturday's game."

She didn't reply. Granted, my small-talk skills weren't great, but she wasn't giving me much to work with.

"You okay?" I asked. Her face looked tired.

"Yeah, I'm fine. I guess."

I pointed my finger in the opposite direction. "Do you want me to leave you alone?"

"What? No, not at all." Her demeanor changed instantly, and she smiled at me. "I'm so sorry, I was just preoccupied with something. How are you doing? Are you excited about Saturday's game?"

"I hope Coach lets me play," I said. "I'm in his bad books again."

We continued walking and talking, mostly about basketball and our favorite teams. Then Nicole did a killer impression of Coach Carter—I had no idea she was so funny—and I realized I had never actually taken the time to get to know her.

I told her about my family, Poppy, and my troubles with Jason. She told me her parents were both in the Navy and their family moved around a lot. Western had been a new school for her too since they'd only moved here from Florida last year.

We stopped walking and leaned against the fence. "It must be tough moving around so much."

She nodded. "That's why I love basketball. There's always a place to shoot hoops around somewhere."

"What was it like to play with the Ravens?"

"I didn't like it," she said, her tone getting more serious. "They definitely lived up to their lousy reputation. That girl Rachel was an absolute nightmare."

"I bet. Is she the reason you left?"

"It was a bunch of things, but she was a big part of it." She paused as if she was deciding whether to confide in me.

I wanted to know what happened, but I didn't want to pressure her.

She took a deep breath. "The whole team is super competitive, and when the coach started giving me more playing time, Rachel got ticked off. She turned the whole team against me and bad-mouthed me around the school."

Her story made me feel ashamed of my own behavior when we first met. I frowned, but in the moment, I didn't really know what to say.

"Rachel even started a rumor that I was a thief and stole money from her." She reached up and fidgeted with her necklace. "It was a total lie, but it got around the whole school. It was impossible to make friends after that."

"I'm really sorry that happened to you, Nicole."

She shrugged her shoulders.

"I love your necklace."

"Thanks," she replied, but immediately stopped playing with it. "My grandmother gave it to me last year.

Just before we moved." She sighed. "And we might have to do it again. My parents are supposed to know by this weekend. I can't stop worrying about it. That's why I've been so spaced out."

"I really hope you get to stay." But I couldn't just leave it at that. If I was going to be honest with myself and my friends moving forward, she deserved an apology from me too. "And..." I stared at the grass, too ashamed to look at her. "I'm sorry... I was a total jerk about the whole shooting guard thing. I shouldn't have made everything about me. I've been almost as bad as—"

BRRINGGGGG!

The end-of-lunch bell rang out before I could say Rachel's name.

"Sorry, what was that last part?" Nicole asked, then winked.

I smiled. It didn't seem worth repeating now. "Nothing. I'm just really glad we're friends now."

"Me too," she said. And we headed back into the school together.

24

NOTHING TO FEAR

After my conversation with Nicole, things were great between us. We even got in trouble for chatting in class, but I could tell Coach Carter was happy we were getting along. He paired us up during practices and worked us harder than we'd ever been worked. Melina was still away, but Siarra and the others players were warming up to me again too.

And at the end of Thursday's practice, Coach thanked everyone for their dedication, then said, "We're *all* ready for Saturday's game," and nodded directly at me.

I pointed at myself and mouthed *me too?*

When he nodded, a huge smile took over my face. "Yes!" I said, pumping my fist. I got to be a part of the team.

I looked up into the stands and smiled. Mom, Dad, and Jason were sitting together laughing and joking around as they watched our game.

Since it was a home game, we had the advantage. *Home.* I loved the word. Home meant you felt safe, secure, comfortable. And, for the first time in a long time, I felt truly safe. About everything. Mom and Dad were happy. Our money troubles were going away. I wasn't even worried about the game.

The Eagles were a solid team that had already made the playoff tournament, so this game wasn't nearly as important to them as it was to us. They still wanted to win, of course, but not as badly as we did.

It was the last quarter and they were leading by only eight points, so it was still anyone's game. Coach called for a time-out and we all huddled near the bench.

"Stick to the plan," he said. "Pay attention to your teammates. Find the pass. Make the play."

"We can still win this," Melina said, shooting me a friendly grin. I was so glad she was back and no longer mad at me.

"And make the playoffs," Siarra added.

"Yeah!" we all cheered.

"And then we can really show the Ravens what we're

really made of," I said, and looked at Nicole. "Right, Nicole?"

Nicole hesitated before nodding, which wasn't the reaction I was expecting. Was she concerned about having to move again, or about playing the Ravens?

Coach looked up from his clipboard. "Let's not get ahead of ourselves." He motioned for us to huddle up even closer. "It's still anyone's game. We need to stay focused on what we can control. Keep working hard and doing your best."

Nicole had been having a pretty good game and had scored twelve points. I'd even scored a few. And I was having so much fun, it didn't even bother me too much that we were behind. Besides, if we ran the plays the way Coach Carter had taught us, we might still come back and win.

But for that to happen, Nicole needed to score more points. I needed to convince her to take the shot. She was still passing too much—almost as if she was afraid we might make the tournament.

The huddle broke up, and I followed her back onto the court. "Nicole," I said, placing a hand on her shoulder. "You're our best shooter. I'm going to set you up, but you need to take the shot. Don't be afraid... You've got this! Take the shot."

She gave me a thumbs-up, and I ran over and took my position.

When play resumed, I did everything I could to ensure she got the ball. Any time I stole the ball from the opposing team, I passed it to her to ensure she was in the best position to score.

And she scored almost every time.

I assisted on every play. I boxed out other players so Nicole could get more rebounds. If I got a rebound on our side, I quickly passed the ball to her and created a fast break. My passes were almost perfect. Precise. Tight. Not too hard, not too soft.

And it wasn't just me and Nicole. Everyone was playing their positions well. We were functioning like a real team and the plays were working.

Then something strange happened. The closer we got to tying the game, the worse Nicole played. Instead of taking the shots we set her up with, she went back to passing. I set her up with two perfect opportunities, but she didn't take either of them.

Fortunately, after a few more minutes of game play, Siarra made a basket and tied the game.

I didn't know if it was intentional or not, but Nicole's head was no longer in the game. If we were going to win, someone else was going to have to score the winning basket. For whatever reason, she just didn't have it in her. She couldn't do it.

With the final minute of the game running out, I gained possession and dashed toward the hoop.

Then something else weird happened: I entered "the zone," that elusive and mysterious state of mind every actor, athlete, and artist talks about. I'd heard about it, but I had never really experienced it myself.

Being in the zone was amazing, but hard to describe. It felt like the split second before splashing into a pool, falling asleep, or getting the giggles. Summer sun. Falling snow. Coasting on a bike. All rolled into one. Basically, it felt like I was the luckiest person in the world and nothing could possibly go wrong. Everything was perfect.

My mind was clear and calm. My heart pumped in my chest as my body moved effortlessly forward. Nothing could stop me. And it was happening just in time, because the final seconds of the game were running out.

If we lost the game, we didn't get to go to the tournament. If we won, we were in. I wanted to win.

I had only one goal. One destination. One target. The basket.

It felt like I was moving at regular speed but everyone else was in slow motion. My eyes locked onto the metal hoop ten feet off the ground. One, two, three strides and I thrust one knee into the air. I lifted up, up and stretched my arm out as far as it would go.

I felt the smooth texture of the ball roll off my fingertips as it flew toward the basket. I watched it hit the exact spot I aimed for on the backboard and bounce into the hoop.

And then I heard the almost deafening sound of the final buzzer go off.

We won the game! We were in the tournament!

Beating the Eagles by only two points was a little too close for comfort. Still, we'd won, *and* I'd helped Nicole get a lot of points. Everything was going according to plan.

Everything but Nicole's strange behavior...

We lined up for quick handshakes with the other team, then gathered at the bench and congratulated each other on the win. After a few minutes, everyone began to collect their things.

"Taylor!" Coach Carter called out to me. "Nice job out there tonight. You're really inspiring the other players."

"Thanks, Coach," I said. "Everyone is working hard, and we're playing really well as a team."

"You sure are. There's just one thing missing."

I gave him a confused look. "What do you mean?"

"You should be wearing this," he said, and tossed me the captain's wristband.

"Really?"

"You've earned it. You've given the team hope. Now they see what they're capable of."

"Do you think we have a shot at winning the tournament?" I asked.

"Don't you see? That doesn't even matter."

"I know, but I still want to win." I grinned at him. "For the name on the front of the jersey!"

He smiled and said, "It's okay to want to win, Taylor, as long as you know it isn't everything."

I nodded, finally understanding what he meant. "I think we've got a good shot," I added. "We're a lot stronger now that we're all working together."

"That's true in basketball and life."

Win or lose, I knew exactly what I had to do. What *we* had to do. We needed to show everyone, including ourselves, who we really were.

And when we walked onto the Ravens home court as a team, that's exactly what we were going to do.

25

VISUALIZE WINNING

We were running drills at the last practice before the tournament when Coach blew his whistle and called us over. Chelsey, the Bruins player who'd given us the speech on basketball and friendship, was standing next to him.

Coach gave her a quick introduction, and she stepped forward.

"First of all..." She paused to applaud. "Congratulations on making the playoffs."

We all cheered.

"I look forward to watching you play this weekend," she continued. "As you know, this year's tournament is being hosted by the Western Elementary School Ravens."

We all booed.

"That's enough!" Coach said.

But Chelsey smiled. "It's okay. A little healthy competition is a good thing."

She went on to explain how the tournament worked. It was single elimination with eight teams and took place over the course of one weekend. There were four games on Saturday, and on Sunday, each of the four winning teams faced off against another winner in the morning. Then, after lunch, the final two teams played for the championship.

"How does that sound?" she asked.

We all cheered again.

"Good. With the last few minutes of practice, we're going to participate in a visualization exercise."

She arranged us into two rows and had us lie flat on our backs and close our eyes. It felt weird, but kind of nice at the same time.

"Now," she said. "I want you to imagine the final game. Visualize it. Picture the scoreboard in your mind. The game is tied at sixty-eight. You look around the school gymnasium and up at its tall ceiling. Pennants and banners celebrating previous victories are hanging down from the ceiling. Listen to the sounds. You can hear fans in the stands whispering."

I did as she instructed, and vivid pictures flashed across my mind.

"You're in the zone. Mind and body are balanced. Thoughts and actions are one. Your mind is clear and calm. Your body is energized and ready. Feel your heart pumping in your chest. Hear your sneakers squeaking against the floor."

As I listened to her words, my mind transported me to an imaginary game.

"The powerful muscles in your arms and legs propel your body forward. Electricity fills the air, creating an eerie sensation. You feel like you can fly. All distractions disappear. Nothing can stop you."

In my mind, my eyes locked onto the orange metal hoop ten feet off the ground.

"The ball is in play. Your teammate passes it to you. It feels good to hold the basketball in your hand. You dribble it down the court. You see an opening and you move into the lane. This is your chance. This is your shot."

As she spoke, my heart started to race and my breathing quickened. The muscles in my whole body tensed.

"You push hard toward the basket and jump. Your body moves up. Extending your arm, you release the ball and watch as it arcs through the air. Everything goes quiet. All you hear is the *swish* as the ball passes through the hoop."

A feeling of joy rushed through my whole body.

"How do you feel?" Chelsey asked.

"Amazing!" I said, unable to contain myself.

The other girls were equally excited and answered in their own words: "Great." "Awesome." "Excited."

I sat up and rubbed my eyes. The other girls were sitting up now too.

"Chelsey has shown us that our thoughts are extremely powerful," Coach said. "But are we going to just sit around and think positive thoughts?"

"No!" I said, getting up off the floor. My teammates followed suit.

"Are we going to wait for the universe to solve our problems?"

"No, Coach!" we said all together.

"What are we going to do?"

"Work, Coach!" we yelled. Coach had asked this question many times before, and we knew the appropriate response.

"And what else?"

"Practice! Practice! Practice!" We chanted in unison.

Coach blew his whistle and practice was over.

Saturday couldn't come fast enough.

26

MESSAGE RECEIVED

Western Elementary looked even more scary and intimidating than before. Even more posters and banners decorated the entrance, and there were so many people—students, teachers, parents, janitors... anyone who had *anything* to do with the school— wearing Ravens jerseys.

Coach had suggested we watch all the games to learn how the other teams played, so I'd asked my parents to drop me off early. I didn't want to miss a single one. Mom and Dad and Jason were going to come back after lunch to watch our first game, which was at 1 p.m. against the Bears.

As I approached the front entrance, I was excited to see that Chelsey was there with the staff from Western Elementary, greeting people.

"Hi, Chelsey," I said. "My name is Taylor, and I'm with the Tigers. You spoke at our school."

She smiled warmly. "I remember. It's nice to see you again, Taylor. Are you excited?"

"Excited and nervous."

"Me too. And I'm not even playing." She had a calm way of speaking that made me feel at ease. "You'll settle in once you get onto the court. Good luck."

"Thank you," I said, and waved awkwardly. There was a line of people waiting and I didn't want to take up too much of her time.

A large schedule was posted high up on the wall behind the registration desk, and the eight teams were lined up in the first row with their game times listed. Underneath, there was a second row with four empty spaces, one for each winner. The third row had two empty spaces. And there was a final spot on the bottom for the winner of the whole tournament.

In addition to the Tigers, the playoff teams were the Ravens, the Falcons, the Bears, the Eagles, the Sharks, the Mustangs, and the Bulls. The first tip-off was at 9 a.m. between the Ravens and the Falcons.

When I entered the gymnasium, the game was in full play and the bleachers were already filled with Ravens fans. There was black and burgundy everywhere I looked.

I climbed to the top row of the bleachers to watch the game, and found myself imagining I was a bird flying high, gliding silently above all the players. Suddenly, the problems that had concerned me so much lately seemed a lot less important.

I hadn't realized that a change in perspective could make such a big difference, but I saw the game more clearly than I ever did before. This wasn't the WNBA. It was just a bunch of kids who loved basketball.

Winning wasn't the right goal after all. Sure, it was fun to win and all—I wasn't going to deny that—but it was also fun to play. It was so simple. How could I have lost sight of it? The answer was right in front of me the whole time. The word *play.*

Unfortunately, this game was turning into the opposite of play. No fun. The Ravens were the defending champions, and Rachel and her teammates had dominated the whole game. I felt bad for the players on the other team. They barely got the chance to shoot the ball —or even touch it.

Rachel threw a few elbows, but never in front of the refs, and she really didn't have to play dirty since the players on the Falcons were no match for the Ravens. They were so intimidated by Rachel, they refused to go up against her. The few times they did get the ball, they threw insane Hail Mary passes from center court.

Thankfully there was very little fouling, so the Falcons were put out of their misery fairly quick.

After the game, Rachel and some teammates found seats on the bleachers a few rows below mine. They were laughing and joking and having a great time.

When I stood up to stretch my legs, Rachel noticed me. But I was wearing an orange and black Tigers jersey, so I was probably pretty hard to miss. She waved, and I smiled and waved back awkwardly, then walked down the aisle to head to the washroom.

Huh. Maybe the Ravens weren't all that bad. Maybe they were just regular kids after all. Maybe Rachel *wasn't* a villain.

Or maybe not.

As I passed by, I noticed Rachel lean over and whisper something to her teammate. They both snickered. Then Rachel smirked at me and said, "Good luck out there."

"Yeah," her friend added. "You'll need it."

"See you on the court," I said defensively and walked away.

"Hey!"

I turned to face Rachel again.

"Tell *Nicole* we said hi."

A chill ran down my spine.

27

FIGHT THE GOOD FIGHT

When Melina and Siarra walked into the gymnasium, we found a secluded spot in the bleachers to watch the next game, which started at 11 a.m. Thankfully, Rachel and her entourage were nowhere to seen.

The second match, between the Eagles and the Sharks, was much more exciting than the first. Both teams played well, and the lead went back and forth in the first half. But the Eagles gained momentum—and kept it—during the second half. They won the game, but only by eight points.

There was a break before the next game, and while we ate our packed lunches, the three of us talked about basketball and school and what we thought high school would be like.

Then Siarra showed us how to do different French

braids and we practiced on each other. It was really fun, like a sleepover. I always thought it was funny that Siarra called them *no*-sleepovers. The sense of friendship and comradery was just like Chelsey had described.

I usually pulled my hair back into a tight ponytail, which gave me a headache if I wore it up for too long. So when Siarra finished putting my hair in a thick French braid, it felt amazing.

Melina was practicing her new braiding skills on Siarra when I noticed Chelsey enter the gymnasium. She was probably super busy with the tournament, but I really wanted to talk with her again, to thank her for visiting our school and let her know I appreciated what she'd said to us.

When Chelsey noticed me approaching, she smiled. "I love your hair."

"Thanks. My friend did it. I'm going to play with it this way."

Chelsey overflowed with kindness as we talked. She was like the amazing big sister every girl wished they had, so smart and funny and confident. It was hard to imagine she'd ever felt anxious or scared.

She even shared some of her personal experiences. A girl once challenged her for her position as center—

they'd hated each other at first—but they'd become best friends. And they were still best friends now.

Would Nicole and I still be friends when we grew up? I hoped so.

Melina and Siarra walked over as Chelsey and I were wrapping up our conversation, and Chelsey said a quick hello to them and wished us good luck.

With lunch break almost over, it was time for us to join Coach Carter and the team. We had a game to win.

As soon as everyone was gathered around him, Coach Carter went over the main plays and gave us a last-minute pep talk. We were up against the Bears, a team with a lot of strong players and a good reputation. Their school had hosted the tournament last year and lost in the finals to the Ravens. I could imagine how badly they wanted to win on the Ravens' home court.

Still, they'd have to get through us first.

Both our teams played really well during the first half, with lots of passing and good ball handling. The lead went back and forth many times.

I set up a lot of good opportunities for us to score, and we capitalized on them. Especially Nicole, but Melina was feeling really good and had scored several times as well.

During the short break before the second half, I looked up at the stands and saw Rachel and her entourage. She was probably just as curious about checking out the competition as I was.

I turned back to my teammates and said, "Let's show them what we're made of." And we did. We pulled ahead and never lost our lead. The Bears were eliminated, and we were advancing to the next round.

Mom, Dad, and Jason ran over and congratulated me, and when we got home, we celebrated with my favorite meal, spaghetti and meatballs.

It was so good to have the whole family together, and Jason seemed like he was in a much better place. He still had some bad habits he needed to break, however.

"I bet no one here can even name three famous women basketball players," he said.

Ugh! Why does he have to ruin everything?

"You're right," Dad replied. "But I can't name three famous mathematicians either. So what?"

"That's different."

"Listen, Jason," Dad said. "Just because things are a certain way doesn't mean they should be."

"Male sports teams get all the attention," I said. "It's not fair."

Dad wiped his mouth with his napkin and nodded. "Then let's work to change it. People will constantly try to tell you what you can and can't do. It's up to you to fight for what you believe in."

"Let's try to get tickets to some of the UCLA women's games," Mom offered.

Jason snorted. "No way! I've watched enough women play basketball this weekend."

I shouldn't have taken the bait, but I totally did, and within seconds Jason and I were arguing loudly. When Baby Gemma started to fuss, my stomach sank. Were we falling into our old patterns? I didn't want anything to jeopardize our rebuilt home.

"I don't want to fight, Jason. Why do we always have to fight?"

"Families fight," Dad said. "Your mom and I fight."

"But it doesn't mean we don't still love each other," she added.

Baby Gemma continued fussing and Dad stood and picked her up from her chair, then held her high and blew a big raspberry on her exposed tummy. She started giggling immediately.

Dad grinned. "We just need to remember what's really worth fighting for."

THE GAME OF OUR LIVES

The next morning, we dropped Baby Gemma off with a friend and headed over to Western Elementary.

Jason gave me his usual "take the shot" advice, but Dad reminded me that as a point guard it was more important to set up the plays. They were both right in their own way, but I would be the one out on the court. Today it was going to be up to me and me alone. And I was ready to take on whatever came my way.

Melina, Nicole, Sienna and I all sat together in the stands for the first game. We watched the Ravens defeat the Eagles by ten points to make it into the final. And when it was the Tigers' turn to play the Bulls, I saw Rachel in the stands watching us. It was a really close game—honestly, it could've gone either way—but we won, which felt great after losing to the Bulls earlier in the season.

Now it all came down to the final game. After lunch, The Ravens and the Tigers would battle it out to see who would be tournament champions.

The gymnasium was packed to capacity. Excited family, students, and fans filled every nook and cranny. Enthusiastic faces of every size, shape, and color stared out from the bleachers. And unlucky latecomers, unable to find seats inside, waited in the hallway.

It was so loud, you had to yell in order to be heard. Even if you were standing right next to the person.

The gym was mostly filled with Ravens fans, but Tigers fans were scattered here and there. It didn't matter to me; my family were the only spectators I cared about. They'd arrived early and had great seats, and even Jason had come to cheer me on again. He'd never admit it, but he was becoming my biggest fan.

The whole gymnasium hushed when Chelsey walked out to center court. She thanked the crowd for coming and explained how the game would play out, then invited everyone to stay after the game for a short ceremony where the winning team would be awarded the championship trophy and the tournament MVP would be announced.

I realized I hadn't thought about being named MVP in weeks. It was no longer important to me. Actually, *winning* wasn't even that important anymore. I still really wanted to beat Rachel, but mostly because of how she'd bullied Nicole.

Rachel had been so mean to her, and for no good reason at all. Jealousy was horrible—and useless. It never helped anything.

I remembered my own feelings toward Nicole when I first met her and felt ashamed. My behavior had been almost as bad as Rachel's.

Thankfully, Nicole and I were past all that now. We had become really good friends. I walked over to her and we bumped fists.

"I love your braids," she said.

"Thanks. I'll do yours after we win."

"You really think we can?" She rubbed her necklace.

I reached over and rubbed her necklace too. "I really do."

Coach called us over, and we got ready to play the game of our lives. In the huddle, he extended a hand into the circle and we placed ours, one at a time, on top. "We got here as a..."

"TEAM!" we shouted in unison.

"We win as a..."

"TEAM!" we yelled, then broke away.

Moments later, the referee tipped the ball... and the game was on.

The Ravens gave us everything they had, and Rachel led the charge. As expected, there was a lot of dirty play. Pinching, pulling, tripping—they even threw the occasional hip check. And they were trash-talking us constantly. Anything to get us off our game.

We took everything in stride, never stooping to their level. And at the halftime break, though the Ravens were in the lead, it was only by six points. It was still anyone's game.

"Win or lose," Coach said, putting his hand in the circle, "do the right thing. Nothing else matters."

We put our hands together and shouted, "One! Two! Three! TEAM!"

We started the second half with possession and put the pressure on immediately. Nicole was like a super-hero, scoring two baskets within minutes. We were closing in on them.

Suddenly, Rachel ran over and said something to the referee. He blew the whistle and called Coach Carter over, and when they both walked over to Nicole, I followed.

"I'm sorry," the referee said. "Jewelry isn't allowed to be worn on the court."

"Seriously?" Coach Carter said, flustered. "You're stopping game play because she's wearing a piece of jewelry?"

"I'm sorry, but I have to follow the rules. Either the jewelry comes off or she does."

Nicole went pale and her shoulders slumped—deflating as if someone had let the air out of her, like a balloon—but she turned around and lifted her hair up. I unclasped the necklace and handed it to Coach Carter.

"Don't worry, Nicole," I said. "You'll get it back right after the game."

But when play resumed, she was out of sorts. She missed an easy layup and then caused a turnover.

Since Nicole was our best scorer, the Ravens did everything they could to shut her down. Every time one of them walked by her, they whispered something. On one play, a girl reached over and pinched her hard, causing Nicole to yelp in pain and snatch her arm away.

I looked around to see if anyone else had noticed. But if they had, no one said anything, especially the referee.

Soon, the Ravens were ahead by eight points, and the possibility of winning the game was slipping through our hands.

The ball went out-of-bounds, and Rachel ran past Nicole. Once again, she said something under her breath to her. And, once again, Nicole was affected by what she heard. I wondered what it could be, but the Ravens scored another basket before I had a chance to figure it out.

On the next play, I gained possession and worked my way to the Ravens basket. I passed Nicole the ball and she went in for a layup. It was a half-hearted attempt, though, and Rachel swatted it away in midair.

Thankfully, Siarra and Melina were each scoring some points for us. But every time I passed Nicole the ball, Rachel shut her down.

I had to do something to help my team—especially Nicole. So I waved to catch Coach's attention and signed for him to call a time-out.

"TIME OUT!" he bellowed, and the ref blew the whistle.

We all ran over to the bench for a quick huddle.

"What's going on?" Coach asked, looking at Nicole. "Are you okay?"

"Maybe you should sub me out. I can't beat Rachel—she's better than me."

"We all doubt ourselves sometimes," I said. "But we haven't lost yet."

"That's right," Siarra added. "Remember what we've done to get here."

Melina smiled encouragingly. "And no matter what happens, win or lose, we do it as a team."

The rest of the players all nodded their heads, but Nicole shook hers. "She's in my head. I don't know what else to do."

I suddenly got an idea. "Coach, let me switch positions with Nicole. It'll take the heat off her."

Coach looked at Nicole. "Are you okay with that?"

"Sure." She shrugged. "It's worth a shot."

The ref blew the whistle. And when the game resumed, the Ravens didn't know what hit them.

Nicole was a quick learner and an excellent point guard. Every time we gained possession, she set me up beautifully. And playing shooting guard felt like coming home. My muscle memory kicked in, and it felt like my body had missed taking shots. My defender was slow, and Nicole and I worked circles around her. I scored again and again and again.

The Ravens tried to put plays together, but we made adjustments and shut them down. Whatever they tried, we countered. We were playing the best game of our lives, and soon we were only down by four points.

Rachel switched places with her teammate so she could cover me.

"Nicole is twice as good as you," she said when she got close. "And even *she* couldn't beat me."

Whenever Jason wanted to really annoy me, he would just smile and laugh. It drove me absolutely insane. So I decided to try it on Rachel. Maybe I could get in *her* head. Besides, I wanted to let her know I wasn't afraid.

I smirked at her and laughed, and her face turned red.

"I'm going to destroy you," she hissed, reaching out her hand out to pinch me.

I slapped it away. "Nope," I said, then laughed again. Her tactics were nothing compared to my big brother's.

I glanced up at the stands, and Jason gave me a thumbs-up and yelled, "TAKE. THE. SHOT!"

When play resumed, Nicole set me up perfectly for two more layups. Unfortunately, Rachel had my number now. She blocked me each time.

I went up for a third time. *THWAP!* She swatted the ball as soon as it left my hand.

"Is that all you've got?" she said. "Weak!"

And in that moment, I realized something: I understood her. Rachel was talented but cocky, smart but brash. She wanted to win for herself, not her team. She was just like me.

Well, just like the old me. She had no idea what the new me was capable of.

She thought she knew everything. That was her weakness. A weakness I could use against her.

I had to keep Rachel focused on me.

"Let's see you try to get past me," I said. "I dare you."

I'd watched both of the Ravens' previous games from the stands, so I knew they rotated through the same few plays every time they got the ball. I'd seen most of their tricks. And since I'd paid extra-close attention to Rachel, I knew she had her own tell. She favored her left side, and her go-to move was fake right then dash left. I just had to be patient.

I kept my eye on her shoulder, and when she made her move, I was right there with her. She had nowhere to go and was forced to pass to another player.

And that's when it happened. Nicole, who was so much faster than the other player, leaped in front of her and intercepted the ball.

Fast break—no one could catch her. Easy layup.

The crowd went wild.

With two minutes left, the Ravens were only up by two points. All we needed was one basket to tie the game. Time slowed down. Seconds seemed like minutes. It was like our whole team was in the zone.

Melina gained possession of the ball and passed to

Siarra. Siarra passed it back to me. I bolted for the basket and stopped just inside the key.

"OPEN!" Melina yelled.

Should I pass her the ball or take the shot?

I launched a chest pass to her and pivoted to block a Raven defender. Melina caught the ball and made a run for the basket. Siarra blocked out another Raven to give Melina more time to take her shot.

Melina stopped, set her feet just like we practiced, and lined up her shot. She released the ball and all eyes in the gymnasium watched as it arched through the air. It soared up, up, up, then reached its apex and floated down—right inside the rim. *Swish!* Nothing but net.

The gymnasium erupted in cheers, and Melina screamed with joy.

The game was tied, but there was no time to celebrate. They had possession. We had to shut them down.

"Full-court press!" I yelled, and we picked up the offensive team right underneath their basket as they tried to inbound the ball. The full-court press was my favorite defense. Fast and frenetic, the pressure and intensity caused a lot of turnovers.

It worked. The Ravens tried to get Rachel the ball, but I was on her like glue. Frustrated, her teammate made a bad pass, and I intercepted the ball.

"Time out!" I yelled, and Coach followed suit. "TIME OUT!"

The game was tied, and we had possession with twenty-six seconds left on the clock. We ran into a huddle.

"We got here as a team," I said. "And we've played the best game of our lives. All we have to do is put the ball in the hoop one more time."

"What's the plan?" Nicole asked, then clapped her hands. "Let's do this!"

Coach Carter smiled at me and winked. "Well, Captain, what do you have in mind?"

I waved everyone in closer. "I'll take shooting guard. Nicole—or whoever—get me the ball, and I'll make a play for the net. Rachel will assume I'm going for the shot. Nicole, you shadow me all the way to the hoop. I'll go up for the shot, but at the last second, I'll pass it back to you."

"Okay," Nicole said, putting a hand on my shoulder. "But if you have the shot, take it!"

We put our hands together and shouted, "One! Two! Three! TEAM!" then jogged back onto the court and took our positions.

For our plan to work, Rachel needed to stay focused on me.

"Me. Ball. Hoop," I said boastfully. "That's how this is going to go down."

Rachel sneered. "In your dreams."

"You think you can stop me?"

"I *know* I can stop you," she replied.

And... she's hooked.

All her attention would be on me now.

The ball was put in motion, and with one arm extended, I kept Rachel at bay and moved into position, then faked left and stormed for the basket. Rachel stuck closer than my shadow. Exactly as planned.

I leaped into the air and felt her long arms extend right up over me. And at the height of my jump, at the last possible second, I threw a no-look pass back to Nicole.

Rachel was so focused on me, she didn't realize what had happened until it was too late. She swung her arm and swiped the air, but there was nothing there to hit.

The ball was already in Nicole's hands.

Rachel and I landed in a tangled mess, and the entire gymnasium shook as the spectators jumped to their feet. Their screams of excitement told me everything I needed to know—Nicole had caught the ball and scored the winning basket with a perfect layup.

We'd won the tournament. And we'd done it as a team.

I quickly rolled away from Rachel and leaped up, sprinting to center court. "We won!" I screamed. "We won!"

Coach Carter and all my teammates were shouting for joy. Ecstatic, Nicole, Melina, Siarra, and I hugged each other, then everyone on the team held hands and jumped up and down at center court. It was hilarious and awesome at the same time.

Chelsey waved her arms at the people in the stands, inviting parents and fans to come celebrate on the court with us.

My family raced down from the bleachers and ran over, and Dad picked me up off the ground and squeezed me tight. Mom gave me a huge hug and kissed the top of my head while Jason stood in front of me, trying to look all serious. "Nice job, Taylor," he said. Then he grinned, pulled me into a giant bear hug, and spun me round and round until he got so dizzy we almost fell down. Amazing.

It was the best day of my life.

And I got to share it with my family and all my best friends.

29

MVP

The team and I stood tall in a straight line at the east side of the gymnasium.

The awards ceremony was about to begin.

Some onlookers still watched from the stands, but a mass of family, friends, and students still filled center court—with Jason and my parents standing front and center, grinning proudly.

To the left of the entrance, tournament organizers had set up three tables. Chelsey stood nearby, holding a microphone. She tapped on it and asked for everyone's attention.

The gymnasium quieted slightly but was still noisy with rustling and soft chattering. Some spectators were still making their way down the bleacher stairs, and more than a few disgruntled Ravens and their families were exiting the gym through the side doors. They weren't going to stay for the ceremony, but I understood. I'd have been disappointed if I hadn't won too.

Chelsey tapped the microphone again, then gave a short preamble thanking a bunch of the organizers and Western Elementary for hosting the tournament. Then, she invited the crowd to give the Ravens a round of applause. And everyone did—though I saw Jason fake clapping and making faces, which was bad sportsmanship but kind of funny.

Finally, after what seemed like an eternity, Chelsey raised her arm and pointed to us. "Ladies and gentlemen," she said, "on behalf of the Junior League Basketball Association, I would like to present this year's tournament winners—the Central Elementary Tigers!"

The crowd at center court burst into applause and we all joined in. Cheers, hoots, and hollers echoed throughout the gym. Jason did a few of those super loud two-finger whistles, but Dad made him stop.

It was wonderful. A little overwhelming, but wonderful. The noise settled down, and eventually, with Coach's encouragement, so did we.

Chelsey called Coach Carter's name, and he walked up, shook some hands, and took the microphone. After a few remarks, he looked toward us. "I want to thank all of you. You've grown as players, and you've shown us what being a team really means. I'm so proud of the work you did this season, and I hope you're all proud of yourself too. You've proven that great things happen when we work together. You're true champions."

The crowd applauded and he handed the microphone back to Chelsey, who cleared her throat and said, "Basketball is a team sport, but each year a single player —one who displays exceptional leadership and ability —is awarded the Most Valuable Player award. And this year's MVP award goes to..."

This was it. The moment I'd been looking forward to since the start of the season. The reason I let myself get obsessed with basketball and put winning above everything else. The reason I was jealous of Jason and Nicole. The reason I lost sight of what's really important.

And standing there with all my friends, in front of my family and my coach, it hit me. Sort of like that "aha" moment I got when I figured out a puzzle or a riddle. *Of course. How could I have not seen it before?*

It all seemed so silly now. It was just a plastic trophy —and it wasn't what I really wanted at all. Everything I *really* wanted was right here, and had been right here the whole season. My family, my friends, and playing the game I loved.

So when Chelsey called out Nicole's name, instead of feeling jealous, I was overwhelmed with waves of positive energy and gratitude. I cheered and clapped along with everyone else, and then Melina and I grabbed Nicole's hands and the three of us jumped up and down with joy.

Nicole had won MVP—and she deserved it. She had overcome a lot this year. She was the best player on our team. And she was my friend.

Melina and I smiled at each other as we watched Nicole accept her award. The girl who deserved it the most had won, and I was truly happy for her.

My family came over, and Mom and Dad gave me another big hug and told me how proud they were.

"Well, *Captain*," Jason said. "Tough break about MVP." He made an exaggerated frowny face. But I could tell he was only teasing, so I smiled and gave him a "What can you do?" shrug—and he just laughed.

Did he actually understand how I was feeling? It seemed like maybe he did. After all, he'd stood where I was now and had heard his name called, twice. I knew he really missed his friends and playing basketball, so hopefully he'd take this time to realize *why* he loved it so much.

We posed for photos with the trophy as a team and as individual players. And after came pictures with parents, hugs with friends, and lots of fist bumps and high fives. Finally, the event began to wind down and people started leaving.

I glanced over at Nicole. She and her parents were talking with Chelsey, and she was beaming. Not only had she won MVP, her parents told her right after that they weren't moving. She would get to stay.

Coach Carter was still talking with some parents, so I waited until they'd finished and walked over to him.

"Coach?" I felt a bit awkward. I wanted to talk to him, but didn't know exactly what I was going to say.

"Congratulations, Taylor. How are you feeling?"

"Good. Really good," I said, feeling calmer. "That's what I wanted to talk to you about."

"Oh?"

"I wanted to thank you for pushing me in the right direction. I know it's not all about trophies and MVP awards and stuff."

"It was my pleasure, Taylor." He gave me wink and added, "But it sure feels good to win, doesn't it?"

I laughed. "Yeah, it sure does."

Coach left, and as I ran over and joined my family, I felt like this was the end of an important part of my life. But also just the beginning.

THE END.

THANK YOU

Thank you for reading *Friendship or Foul Play*, the fourth book in my Step-by-Step series. I hope you enjoyed Taylor's story as much as I enjoyed writing it. If you did, please share it with a friend. You can also help by leaving a review online to help others discover my writing. It really makes a difference.

Thanks again for reading. You can find all my books at PaulBreau.com

Sincerely,
Paul

ALSO BY PAUL BREAU

Step-by-Step series

Siarra Jones: Skating Into Trouble
Jake Murphy: The Karate Choke
Friendship or Fame: Mia Finds Her Voice
Friendship or Foul Play: Taylor Takes Her Shot

Turn the page to read an excerpt from *Jake Murphy: The Karate Choke*

JAKE MURPHY: THE KARATE CHOKE

Choke and Die of Embarrassment

I couldn't breathe. When I stood up from my desk, my legs were heavy and my head felt light. I looked ahead to the front of the classroom and walked up the aisle. Everything moved slowly, like I was walking through water.

Was that my heartbeat? Why was it going so fast? Should it be taking this long to get to the front of the class?

Oh no! I think I have to pee!

I finally made it to the teacher's desk and slowly turned to face the class—then froze completely, unable to speak. I felt hot, too hot. Sticky hot.

Say something!

Why was I just standing there? Why was I sweating so much? Why was I so *gross*?

I couldn't think straight. Couldn't breathe. Couldn't move.

What's happening? Something's wrong! I'm going to die... I am dying!

If you've ever heard the phrase "deer in the headlights," that was me. My name is Jake Murphy, and up until this moment, I was considered the smartest kid in Ms. Hardish's fifth grade class. That, however, was about to change. I was about to get run over by a giant truck called Anxiety.

I'd had panic attacks before, but never like this. And I'd never had trouble speaking in front of the class. In fact, I usually got into trouble for talking *too* much. So, none of this made any sense.

Ms. Hardish's sweet voice called out, "Jake, we're ready for you. You can start any time."

I'd studied. I knew this stuff. *Come on, man, you're ready!*

But I wasn't ready. I was anything *but* ready. And it didn't matter what I said to myself, I was stuck. Frozen.

"Choke!"

I recognized that sour voice immediately. It came from the meanest kid in my class, my archnemesis, "Mean Dean."

And he was right. I *was* choking. Badly. I was choking like no one had ever choked before. Great! I was going to be the first kid to choke and die of embarrassment.

Choke. That's the word people use when you were supposed to be able to do something, but when the time came to do it, you couldn't. As if I didn't have enough problems trying to survive fifth grade, now I couldn't talk or move. I was petrified!

I'd learned the word *petrified* when my family drove to North Dakota last summer. It was when a living tree turned into a rock, a real thing from the dinosaur age. The word's also used to describe someone who's really, really scared. When someone's so frightened they can't even move.

So not only was I choking, I was officially petrified.

Was this what comedians meant when they talked about "dying on stage"?

Well, I was no comedian, and this was not funny. I'd practiced my report at home all week. I knew it backward and forward. I'd memorized every word, every paragraph, every dramatic pause. I had even come up with some jokes.

But when my turn came, I forgot everything.

Every.

Single.

Thing.

I couldn't remember a word. Not one sentence, not one silly little joke. I couldn't even remember what I was supposed to talk about.

I looked around the class at all the blank faces staring back at me. My eyes got watery. It was like I was sinking in quicksand and was looking for something, *anything*, to stop me from going under.

Don't cry. Don't cry. Don't—

"Jake," Ms. Hardish said gently, looking down at her list. "You were going to tell us about fossils? You can start anytime now . . ."

Nothing. Even with Ms. Hardish's reminder, I had nothing. Nada. Zilch. Zero. And that was exactly what I was going to get on this assignment, zero. Because *I* was a zero. A zero who just stood there like a zombie. Then again, at least zombies could grunt and say "brains." I couldn't even do that!

Mean Dean mimicked the sound of radio static. "Earth to Jake," he said. "Come in, Jake."

Ugh! I hated him so much! Why couldn't he just leave me alone?

Dean was the type of kid that laughed when someone fell and hurt themselves. Dean was the type of kid that would take your cap and throw it in a tree for no reason. The type of kid that came up with mean nicknames for everyone. Yep, you guessed it. Dean and I went all the way back to kindergarten.

"That's enough!" Ms. Hardish gave Dean a stern look, then turned back to me with an encouraging smile. "Take your time, Jake."

As I stood there, trying to unfreeze, Dean coughed "choke" under his breath. Then his little henchmen, Lenny and Shawn, joined him and they all started coughing the word. Soon it felt like the whole class was doing it.

"Choke, choke, choke," they quietly chanted.

But Ms. Hardish came to my rescue. "ENOUGH! The next person who speaks out will be sent to the principal's office."

The whole class went silent. Unfortunately, I remained silent as well.

Silent in English.

Silencio in Spanish.

Silencieux in French.

You can see why I was considered the smart kid in class. The other kids called me "the Brain" behind my back (and sometimes right to my face). I loved learning about new cultures and new languages. I loved words—words were my specialty. Not today.

Tears welled up in my eyes again. This was not good. Freezing in front of the whole class was bad enough, but crying? I would never live it down! Funny, this thought did *not* make me feel any better. Usually, my mind was my safe space. My thoughts were like good friends. Loyal, reliable, helpful, like my best friend, Matt.

Why was I such a jerk? Matt had wanted to do the presentation with me. But *no*, I had to be the smart guy, had to do the presentation all by myself. *Nice job!*

My brain seemed determined to make a bad situation worse. I wiped my eyes. I was able to move again, but my hands were shaking. *Thanks for nothing, brain.*

Wait. Did I hear something? I recognized that name . . .

"Jake?" Ms. Hardish called out my name again.

I didn't respond.

"Jake?"

I still didn't respond. I was stuck inside my head. It was not a pleasant place to be.

Way to ruin your life, Jake.

After what seemed like hours, Ms. Hardish walked over to me. And judging by the worried expression on her face, I must have looked pretty bad. "It's okay, Jake. You can try again later," she said softly, then took me by the hand and helped me through the aisle.

Dean said "Choke!" under his breath as we walked past his desk. He just couldn't resist the urge to make fun of me. He couldn't resist the urge to make fun of anyone, ever.

"Dean!" Ms. Hardish snapped. "I'll see you after class."

"It's just a joke," he said. "Sheesh, lighten up already."

I collapsed into my seat and put my head in my hands.

No doubt about it. Worst. Day. Ever.

To read what happens next, order your copy of *Jake Murphy: The Karate Choke* today.

ABOUT THE AUTHOR

Paul lives in Vancouver, British Columbia, with his wife, daughter, and a Chihuahua dog, named Poppy.

Paul loves books, movies, comics, and video games —essentially, he's still a kid at heart. He also enjoys skating, karate, and drawing.

Paul completed a BA in English Literature from the University of British Columbia.

If you enjoy Paul's books, the best way to keep up with his work is to join the Paul Breau reader list at PaulBreau.com

Made in the USA
Las Vegas, NV
27 December 2022

64218601R00118